Kandi

ISBN: 978-1-950381-13-5

Printed in the United States by
Piscataqua Press
www.piscataquapress.com

Kandi

by Royaline B. Edwards

Dedication

Kandi is dedicated to the Sims Family Reunion. In the early 19th Century, Samuel Sims and Malinda jumped the broom, against the backdrop of Georgia's fiery red clay and backbreaking sharecropping, under post-slavery conditions—setting the stage for this seventh generation's Forty-third Family Reunion. Fictional characters and plots have been used to highlight a few real incidents.

A New Beginning

The air was filled with excitement. I stood in awe of the shiny, black engine puffing billows of black and white smoke; smoke that formed odd funny shapes that floated and blended into the blue sky. My imagination was on the loose. Suddenly, a booming voice rang out, "All Aboard!"

"Kandi!' my mother said, tightening her grip on my hand. Her other hand gripped the large colorful bag we all knew as her *survival* bag. "Hurry, it's time to board the train."

The long platform looked like it had no end. Ahead, I saw Daddy trying to balance Ray-Jay, my three-year old brother in one arm, while he carried an old tattered suitcase—tied with extra rope. A man wearing a red cap walked close behind Daddy pulling a wagon piled high with our trunk, suitcases, and two of Mama's hat boxes teetering on top. Daddy told me later the man was a *Red Cap*. My 14-year-old sister, Elsie, was holding tightly to Rickey, my nine-year-old brother, with one hand, and in the other, the big shoebox filled with food for the long trip to Ohio.

Earlier that morning, Mama had fried chicken, baked biscuits, sliced the pound cake she had baked the day before, and made peanut butter sandwiches. We were the Kane family on our way to Columbus, Ohio from Granville, Georgia. It was June 1, 1943; I was seven years old.

By the time we got to the *Colored* section of the train, my feet were hurting in my new, black patent leather shoes. They were my first store-bought shoes; the little pinch I felt when I tried them on went away when I squeezed my toes a bit. I couldn't bear to leave those pretty shoes in the store.

"All Aboard!" shouted the booming voice again. Only this time, it was right in front of me. Seeing first his shiny black shoes, I slowly looked up to the giant looming over me. I blinked at the bright gold buttons that stood out against his black suit and black hat. He waved us on board. Scared and excited at the same time, I stared at the long aisle of seats on both sides. Passengers were twisting, smiling, and waving to people outside their windows.

Daddy boarded the train, and the man wearing the red cap helped him fit our other suitcases in the rack above the double seats he had saved for us. Ray-Jay was like a jumping bean, popping up and down from seat to seat. I wanted to sit next to the large window, but Elsie and Rickey got there first, so I sat between Mama and Elsie, while Ray-Jay sat between Daddy and Rickey. Patting my hand gently, Mama whispered, "This is a long trip, you'll get a turn at the window."

Suddenly, the train jerked and started moving slowly, then stopped again. "What happened, Mama?"

I asked, feeling nervous.

Daddy smiled and said, "Don't worry Kandi, once the train starts to move and builds up steam, the outside world will rush by like a picture show." And, sure enough, it did.

I settled back in my seat imagining those big iron wheels speeding over the many miles of railroad tracks taking us far away from Georgia. After a while, Mama started humming a little fast tune. When I looked up at her, her eyes were closed, and her face kept changing—sometimes happy, sometimes sad. Then she started swaying her body from side to side to the beat of the song she was humming. I didn't want her to catch me staring, so I touched her arm gently. She stopped humming, opened her eyes slowly, then looked down at me and smiled.

"Mama," I asked, "what's the name of that song you were humming. It's pretty." She didn't answer at first, just smiled and looked at Ray-Jay, curled into a little ball on Daddy's lap, and Rickey and Elsie taking turns on each other's shoulders. All were napping.

"Great Day! Great Day!" Mama said, turning to me. Her voice sounded a little strange, and her eyes were kind of watery. I was about to ask her what was the matter when she said, "That's the name of the song. It's a spiritual our ancestors sang long ago. And it is a great day, Kandi, even though I am feeling both sad and happy."

"I don't understand," I said. "How can you mix happy and sad together? Is it like mixing sugar and salt?" I wondered if they would taste good or yucky together.

Mama said, "It's hard to compare things outside the body with feelings that are inside the body. Happy and sad are feeling words, and there are times when the two become entangled or mixed up with each other—like when you want to laugh and cry at the same time. We grownups call it mixed emotions." Mama stopped talking and hugged me close.

"It *is* a great day, Kandi, because our family is leaving the south, a place that chipped away a part of me every time I would see the *White Only* signs in the windows of public restaurants, or public buildings—like the library, waiting rooms at train and bus stations, or benches in public parks or other public places—all of which we are taxed to help maintain, but can't use. Also, the outdated school textbooks often sent to our schools, while the newest editions go to the white schools first." Pausing, Mama said softly, "I am also sad because we're leaving your Grandpa and Granny, aunts, uncles, cousins, and friends. Saddest of all, I'll miss my birthplace, Georgia: its chalky red clay, Stone Mountain, clear running brooks and streams, draping magnolia and weeping willow trees—all God's creations for all living beings to respect and enjoy."

Mama's talk made me think of the times when I would overhear grownups fuss about somebody called Jim Crow, and what a sin and a shame how he wanted to keep black people *in their place*.

I looked at Mama and asked, "Is sin and shame

about not liking people because they look different?"

Mama said, "That's a tough question to answer right now, Kandi. Let's put it on the shelf until later."

"But Mama," I said, feeling sadness in my chest, "why don't white people like us? Did we do something bad to them?"

Mama's face made those changes again. Then she said softly, "Not all white people hate or dislike black people because of our color. The same is true of black people in their feelings about white people. We must remember..."

Ray-Jay's *um hungry song* interrupted our talk. It was time to eat. Soon, people were taking down and opening shoeboxes, fat brown grocery bags, and croaker sacks. One family had a big picnic basket.

Daddy laughed and said to Mama, "It won't be long before this car smells like Aunt Susie's kitchen..."

"Like when she's frying up a batch of chicken for the church supper," Mama said, smiling and giving me the look that our talk was on the shelf.

Soon the sky grew dark. Out came tiny, twinkling stars popping out like far-away firecrackers; we all settled in our seats for sleeping the best we could. I tried, but my wide-awake eyes, dilly-dallying with my mind, made it flip flop from one image to another until I was back in Georgia overhearing Daddy say to Mama, "It's time to tell the kids, Fannie."

Mama had sighed and said, "Yes, James, I know, but I wish we didn't have to go. Papa and Granny are getting up in age, and I just hate moving so far away."

"I do, too," Daddy said, *"but I got another letter from Ben that his boss still wants to hire me. You know I would never get such a job down here."*

That's how I found out we were moving up north, and it had made me sad.

The train's whistle jolted me back to the present, and somewhere between the jolt and the clickety clack of those big wheels taking us farther away from Georgia, I fell fast asleep.

The next morning, my wake-up call was the warm sun beaming down on my face. Mama and Daddy were busy gathering our belongings, while Rickey and Ray-Jay were yawning and stretching from the uncomfortable ride through the night. People rushed about getting their things and heading for the door. Pulling down our last suitcase, Daddy said, "Wait here while I go look for a Red Cap." I plopped down near a window because my feet were beginning to hurt.

"Look!" shouted Rickey. Ray-Jay ran to the window, stepping on my foot.

"Mama, Mama," Ray-Jay howled, "train on fire!" On a nearby track was a train swooshing puffs of white and gray smoke from below.

"Oh, Ray-Jay, Mama said, hugging him. "That's just the train letting off steam. In a few minutes, we'll be in the waiting room." Satisfied there was no fire, Ray-Jay began his *Um hungry song.*

Daddy returned with a Red Cap, and, with his help, we made it off the train. I looked down at my pretty black patent leather shoes, and with every step, wished

I could kick them off, freeing my crowded toes.

Once inside, I hobbled as fast as I could to a row of empty seats and tried slipping my feet free, but they would not bulge.

"What's the matter?" Mama asked, taking something from her survival bag. Daddy, seeing my tears, sat next to me and wiggled my feet free. He then hurried to one of the ticket windows for information about our next train. Mama looked at me, smiled and handed me my old shoes.

"Mama, You didn't throw them away!" Everybody watched as I slipped my feet easily into my old, throw-away shoes and pranced around like a princess. I looked up to see Daddy rushing toward us, and he didn't look happy.

"Okay," he said. "Our train is on track twelve, and we need to board now!"

It wasn't long before the Red Cap, with our suitcases piled high on his wagon, was zigzagging through the crowd, far ahead of us. All of us knew where we needed to be with each other. With so many people rushing about, it was hard keeping the Red Cap in sight. We finally boarded the Baltimore and Ohio train that would take us to our new home.

I nearly tripped over Mama's big survival bag, rushing to get the window seat. Rickey pouted, but Mama reminded him that he'd had his turn. I glued my face to the big, wide window, in wonder of the picture frames that moved quickly by.

"Mama! Daddy! Look at all the pretty houses and

barns. I thought of asking Mama for my pad and pencil, but I didn't want to miss anything!

Morning tiptoed into the quiet afternoon. Somewhere in between, I fell asleep. When I woke up and looked around, I tugged Mama's sleeve, pointing to the new people sitting in the seats across from us. I whispered, "Mama, look!"

Mama smiled and said quietly, "This train is headed north, and we are now over the Mason Dixon Line and can sit anywhere we like."

"Where is the line? Can I see it? Is it painted on the roads?" I asked, wondering how big and long it was. Mama was about to explain when we heard the booming voice of the conductor, "Next stop, Columbus!"

Mixed Emotions

Uncle Ben met us at the train station and, after several attempts to fit our belongings into and on top of his old, cranky station wagon, we were finally on our way. Daddy said later that Ray-Jay, Rickey, and I fell asleep like dominoes.

"We're here," Mama said, gently shaking us awake. It took almost as much time getting out of Uncle Ben's station wagon as getting from the train station!

Everything looked and felt strange to me. What funny-looking houses, I thought to myself. "Uncle Ben," I said, "why are the houses stuck together?"

He laughed and said, "These are row houses."

"Why are there so many of them?" I asked, shifting from one foot to the other in my comfortable old shoes. "Which one do you live in?" Before he could answer, a door opened and there stood Aunt Sadie, Mama's oldest sister.

"Lordy, me!" she said. "Here you are. Come on in. I got food waiting 'cause I know some little tummies are growling aplenty." Once we were inside, she locked the screen door. Then, spreading her big, long arms wide, she gathered us kids into them—giving us tight hugs and kisses on our forehead. Letting go, she said, "Stand back and let me look at you young'uns." Ray-Jay and Rickey stared at Aunt Sadie, with side glances at all the fixings on the table. After the blessing of the food by Uncle Ben, our growling tummies were soon full and happy. Later, Aunt Sadie led us upstairs to the space our family would share until we could find a place of our own.

After two weeks of house hunting, Daddy and Uncle Ben found a rent house about four blocks away. It was a five-room, shotgun duplex that we all had a hard time fitting into. We were happy until those pests showed up. Mama soon declared war on those critters, and, before long, anywhere possible for them to gnaw their way in was plugged with tin can tops. We kids were given strict orders to leave no food around, to get them liking us.

Settling In

Our small backyard had a fence that separated us from an old two-story barn. It had a long path that led to a big brown house. I liked the old barn, with its shiny red paint, and two big doors held together with a big black latch. I wasn't sure about the open hayloft; it made me a little nervous.

One day, Rickey and I were playing near the fence. With a grin on his face, he pointed to the hayloft. "Kandi," he said slyly. I betcha you can't jump from that hayloft."

Seeing Mamma at the window, I said, "I betcha you're about to be in big trouble."

Mama rushed out, caught our attention and whispered, "Kandi, you and Rickey stay away from that fence! White folks live there, and we don't want trouble." I wondered why Mama was whispering—no one else was around. Besides, I knew who lived there. It was a girl about my age, with red hair; she was playing near the brown house the day we moved in.

Mama was right about changes we would have to get used to, and it seemed new ones popped up every day. September brought a big one.

It was day three and Ray-Jay stood in the middle of

the floor screaming, "I don't wanna go!" He didn't like being dropped off at Aunt Sadie's for the day, since Mama had found a job. Suddenly, he stopped screaming. You could hear a pin drop. At the door was Mama with *The Look;* it meant the end of the hugs and cuddling Ray-Jay had settled for. For the rest of the week, his screaming turned into a little whine that we could all live with.

Finally, we all knew where we were supposed to be for the day, starting with Daddy leaving for work before the break of day, Rickey and I taking the school bus, and Elsie riding the city bus to the high school.

Now, the strangest feeling for me was the first day of school—none of my teachers had brown skin! Before leaving Georgia, we were told how different our lives would be in a big city up north. I could not believe my eyes when the teacher gave us school supplies, along with new books! We even had different teachers for art, gym, and music. In Georgia, our small elementary school had one teacher for each grade up to fifth grade. They taught everything!

At recess time, my joy faded when I saw the big playground with swings, see-saws, something called monkey bars, and spaces to play hopscotch. I searched for Rickey's face, but he was nowhere to be seen. I learned later there were two playgrounds—one for boys and one for girls. Back home, we all played together.

I was feeling sad and alone, until a gentle hand rested on my shoulder. With relief, I looked up into the smiling face of my teacher, Miz Dalton. Standing next to her was a girl with a friendly smile. Miz Dalton said, "This is Sarah, our classroom helper this week. She will show you around the playground and where to line up when the bell rings."

Sarah took my hand and said, "Let's race to the swing set." She let go my hand. "Come on Kandi, there's only one swing left!" Sarah was a talker, but being shy, I didn't mind at all. I liked the sound of her words. Next, we raced to the teeter-totter and was about to jump on when a girl with red hair came over.

"Hi Penny," said Sarah. "Want to play with us?"

Penny and I stared at each other. Feeling nervous, I said, "Hi," but she didn't say hi back. Instead, she ran and jumped on the teeter-totter. I watched as she and Sarah bobbed up and down laughing and talking so fast, I could hardly keep up with what they were saying. I guess my ears will have to learn to listen faster, I laughed to myself.

When they got off, Penny looked at me and asked, "What's your name?"

"Kandi," I said in my slow, southern drawl. She giggled. After that, my tongue glued itself to the roof of my mouth for the rest of recess. That evening, I drew pictures of my first day at school

Neighborly Encounters

One Saturday, when Rickey and I were playing near the fence Mama had warned us about, a boy and girl came out of the big brown house and started running down the path toward the barn. When they saw us, they stopped and stared. We stared back. I turned to leave, but stopped. It was the girl's red hair—It *was* Penny!

"Hi Kandi," she said moving closer to the fence. She remembered my name, I thought.

Looking at Rickey, the boy asked, "What's your name?"

"Rickey."

"I'm Seth. Wanna play?" he asked.

"Play what?' Rickey answered, eyeing me and slowly moving away from the fence.

"Hide and Seek," he said.

"Where?" asked Rickey.

"There," he said, pointing to the barn.

Grinning, Penny whispered to me, "I know places to hide where they will never find us, especially in the loft."

I wanted to say I didn't want to play in that scary loft, but the words got stuck on my tongue.

"I don't know," Rickey said slowly. "My mama told

us to stay on this side of the fence 'cause we don't want trouble."

I was waiting for Penny and Seth to giggle at Rickey's southern talk. They didn't, but before we could decide on the hide-and-seek thing, Mama came to the door, gave us *The Look* and said it was time to eat. While we didn't play that day, we would in days to come, and also become friends.

It was Saturday, and the *thu-bump, thu-bump* of our second-hand Maytag washer meant it was wash day.

I got up, peeked out the window, and watched the clothes on the clothesline swaying in the breeze. In my head, I put heads and limbs on some of the clothes and was about to get my drawing pad when, from outside, I heard an unfamiliar voice.

"I guess you might say we're *backyard* neighbors. I'm Mary Anderson, Seth and Penny's mom."

"Nice to meet you, Mrs. Anderson," Mama said slowly.

"Oh, please, call me Mary," she answered.

Stumbling a bit, Mama said, "I-I'm Fannie Kane."

"Well, it's nice to meet you, Fannie. Seth and Penny are always talking about Rickey and Kandi. Moving closer to the fence, she said, "Today, I baked cookies for Seth's Boys Scout Troop, and, after putting the last batch in the oven, I saw you at the clothesline, and thought I would welcome you to the neighborhood with these." She handed a covered dish to Mama.

"Why that's mighty nice of you to do that, Miss,

uh...Mary," Mama said, smiling and looking surprised at the same time. Once those cookies were on our kitchen table, they flew off that plate like they had wings!

Snow Drifts

Time passed quickly. One morning, I woke up to the most beautiful sight. Outside, everything was shiny white! Rooftops were piled high with soft, white snow, while tree limbs bowed gently under the burden of it. This was my first time seeing so much snow, and I could hardly wait to get out in it—and I did.

"Kandi!" Mama shouted, standing at the door shaking. "Don't you know you can't play outside dressed that way? This is not Georgia!"

"It's fun, Mama." Gathering handfuls, I threw the snow up, letting it fall around me. A few days later, I was tucked snuggly under heavy quilts, with cod liver oil, Vicks Salve, and taking some nasty-tasting stuff in a brown bottle, called *Father John*.

Mama tried to convince me it would help shoo my cold away, but I wasn't sure about that at all!

It seemed a hop, skip, and a jump that winter soon gave over to spring, and the news that our dream had come true. Uncle Ben found a bigger house for rent on Parker Street. We were all very excited. I didn't say much because I felt a little sad thinking about leaving my new friends and the old barn—now a favorite place to play.

When we saw the size of the house, there was much oohing and aahing, squirming and giggling and wondering why it was taking so long for Uncle Ben to park the car. Once inside, we all claimed our own little territory, especially the large fenced-in backyard. Later, as we were getting into Uncle Ben's car for the drive home, I looked up to see a man's face disappear from the upstairs window of the house next door.

A few weeks later, the new-house "bubble" popped liked a balloon, shattering dreams of happiness for our family. We were told the neighbor next door complained he didn't want a bunch of noisy kids living next to him. Sometime later, we found out the real reason, when Uncle Ben came over to return Daddy's deposit money.

"I'm sorry things didn't work out about the house," Uncle Ben said. "But you know how it is in this country."

"Yeah, I know," said Daddy in a voice that sounded more sad than angry. "I thought it might be different here, but not much. It's just not as full in your face as it is down south." Uncle Ben walked over to where Daddy was seated, patted him on the shoulder and left.

Everybody found something to do after saying good-bye to Uncle Ben. Mama started dinner, Rickey took Ray-Jay for a ride in his new wagon, and Elsie turned on the radio to listen to *The Shadow*. I went for my pad and pencils.

When I got back, Daddy was slumped on the davenport, his head resting on the back, his eyes closed. I wanted to do something so his sad and happy feelings wouldn't get all mixed up like Mama's. It was hard for me to understand that the reason we didn't get the house was more about the color of our skin than just being normal people happy and excited about having a bigger and nicer place to live. I hoped my pictures would cheer Daddy up.

The next day was a rainy Saturday. The smell of bacon meant Mama was making our favorite breakfast, after getting Daddy off to work at his part-time job.

Mama said, "We were all disappointed about yesterday, but I don't want you kids to feel you did something wrong. After taking the hot biscuits from the oven, she said, "I have a story to tell you about your Uncle Tripe after breakfast."

Rickey and I asked, "Does he get into trouble?"

"Wait and see," said Mama. She pulled up the usual high stool she used when reading or telling us stories.

"Mama," said Elsie. "Since I already know most of Uncle Tripe's childhood adventures, I'll take Ray-Jay to visit Aunt Sadie." Mama was a good storyteller, and Rickey and I didn't mind, especially since it was a rainy day.

At first, Mama didn't say anything—just looked at us with a smile. She brought her hands together, locking her fingers, then, slowly opening them, as the signal to begin a once-upon-a-time story. "Now," she said, "let's travel back for a short family history lesson."

Mama's Story

A long time ago, when my grandparents, Samuel Smith (Paw Paw) and Viola Simmons (Granny Vee), *jumped the broom*, meaning got married, they had a large family—six sons and four daughters. They lived in a big farm house that sat on 24 acres of land, and whenever a son *jumped the broom*, he and his bride were given a piece of it, once a new Smith baby was on the way. John, my daddy, was their fifth child. He *jumped the broom* with my Mama, Sally Blanton, and it wasn't long before there were three of us: Sadie, Tripe, and myself.

Our land was a long walk from Paw-Paw and Granny Vee's farmhouse, but Tripe and I didn't mind, if it was a warm, sunny day, and Mama said we could go. One day, we were about half way there when Tripe shouted, "Look, Fannie!" Turning in the direction he was pointing, I was surprised to see a little brook that led to a clump of small trees.

"Come on Fannie," he said, his eyes bright with mischief when he wanted to do something he shouldn't. "We're not too far from Paw-Paw and Granny Vee's. It could be a short cut, with some juicy blackberries along the way." Not really wanting to, I left the path and followed Tripe until we got to the trees.

"I don't think I want to go in there," I said, standing back. Tripe grabbed my hand and pulled me along.

"Don't be so scared, Fannie. I'll protect you."

We followed the little brook until we got to a big open space. There was a small lake with water so clear you could see your face in it.

"Sure wish I could swim," Tripe said, inching closer to the bank.

"Come on Tripe, let's go."

"I watched cousins Jonathan and Thomas at the old mill pond last week, and swimming looked kinda easy. Wanna try it?"

"No!" I said, now getting scared. "There could be a monster down there." Pulling Tripe by the arm, I said, "Let's go back home." At the mention of a monster, Tripe backed away. "We can tell Mama we changed our minds about going to Paw-Paw and Granny Vee's."

Turning to leave, a big swooshing sound made us look back to see a huge stream of water spouting from the middle of the lake. Feeling wetness from the spray of the water, I started running and screaming, "Come on, Tripe!"

I didn't know Tripe could run so fast. He whizzed by me like Flash Gordon, and was on the path heading home by the time I was half there. So much for protecting me, I thought, trying to catch up with him.

Leaving out the swimming part, we told Daddy and Mama about our little adventure at the supper table.

In a stern voice, Daddy said, "That lake is not a

place for you two. It's pretty, but dangerous. You can't swim, and there are water moccasins aplenty, and Lord knows what else. It's time you two have more chores to do."

Missing Daddy's warning tone, Tripe said, "We can learn to swim, and I'm not afraid of snakes."

"You speak for yourself, Tripe," I said, giving him the eye about the part of the story we left out. From that day on, I was happy to help my older sister Sadie gather eggs from the henhouse, learn how to churn butter, and later how to knit and sew.

Each passing year brought its special ups and downs to large and small country families. We planted and harvested vegetable gardens, fruit orchards, sewed most of our own clothes—often passed down through several generations. Younger kids watched while older siblings designed and completed scooters and wagons from worn-out wheels, discarded crates, and unearthed artifacts from the nearby junkyard. Others found joy in fishing and hunting. In late fall, every six to sixteen year old Smith trudged to the one-room schoolhouse for the 3Rs, based on Granny Vee's conviction that once we had them inside our heads, we would be on the road to freedom.

Sunday, considered our rest day, was way out of step, to our way of thinking, because we had to go to Little Zion Baptist Church to listen to Rev. Joshua Johnson.

His preaching, slow and deliberate, often began with "Brothers and sisters, we have to keep the faith and love everybody, if we want a place in heaven."

About an hour later, his heavy voice would increase in volume and tempo, jolting awake all nappers and snoozers like us kids.

We're tired of being under bondage like the children of Israel! How much longer do we have to wait to enjoy the freedom to get good jobs and live wherever we wish? How much longer do we have to wait before we are free to go to the polls and vote without fear for our lives? We are all human beings, with God-given rights, before we are anything else.

Those words meant he was on his way to what we called whoopsville.

Most of the grown-ups began answering back with loud voices of, "Amen! Amen!" Sister Nellie Johnson would whip out her *Gospel Pearl* song book, followed by others, and before long, shouts and shouting filled the church.

Sister Cordelia Walker, seeing those *Gospel Pearl* books, would make her way to the old, tired, worn-out, hand-me-down piano. She would slowly touch a few keys, and suddenly those tired, cotton-picking fingers would fly over them like birds flying over a cornfield. At last, we kids were free to move our bodies from side to side, clap our hands and tap our feet to the music.

The service ended when Deacon Dan Beaver, in his closing prayer, reminded everyone to send up their timbers to the Lord each day and have faith that life would soon get better for us all. That faith would be put to the test years later.

Time brought tears of joy at new births and tears of sorrows at deaths. In 1913, we gathered to say farewell to Paw-Paw and Granny Vee. They passed away within three days of each other. Granny Vee of a broken, weakened heart, after Paw-Paw succumbed to pneumonia.

Feeling Mama was near the end of her story, I said, "Mama, I think I know now how sadness and happiness can get mixed up." It's like when we are born, there is happiness, but underneath is sadness because the newborn will grow up like us, wondering how long it will take to be really free in our country.

A New Encounter

The next day at school, Penny was absent, and I didn't feel like playing with anyone else, so I just walked around for a while before going to a bench to sit down.

Then, into my life came Jessie Mae Monroe. She was bouncing a ball on the concrete walkway, seeming to have fun alone. I walked toward her. Looking up, and in a familiar southern drawl, she asked in a friendly, but sort of loud voice, "What's your name?" I was so surprised, I stammered, as usual, when nervous.

She giggled and said, "Cat got your tongue, or you forgot your name?"

Slowly, I said, "Kandi."

"What's your last name?" she asked, smiling.

"Kane," I said quietly.

"Do you get hung on the tree at Christmas time?" she asked, giggling hard.

I looked at her with bucked eyes, and, to my surprise, I started giggling, too. I sat on the bench, but Jessie kept right on bouncing the ball. Between bounces, she said, "I'm from Slocomb, Alabama. My mama is picking me up after school today, since it's my first day. I'm in third grade, and, my big sister, Louise is still in Alabama."

I wanted to tell her I liked how she bounced the ball and that she was funny in a nice way, but the bell rang and we ran to line up.

"See ya at the bus stop tomorrow," she said, running to get in the third-grade line.

The next day, at the bus stop, Mr. Polk, our driver, was pulling away. I looked out the window and saw Jessie Mae running, waving her hand.

"Stop!" I said. "Jessie Mae is coming. She's new." Mr. Polk stopped the bus and opened the door.

"Good morning," he said. "Welcome aboard, Jessie Mae. Thanks to Kandi you made it in the nick of time."

Jessie, out of breath, said, in her slow drawl, "Good morning y'all. I'm sorry I'm late, but my clock forgot to do that shake and wake thing."

Penny, sitting next to me, giggled. That started more giggles. Just about everybody on the bus came alive! All except Johnny Jackson. He was sitting on the backseat by himself, his usual mean look, daring anyone to sit next to him. When his friend, Dylan Davis wasn't around, he used hurtful words that made kids cry. I was hoping Jessie Mae would find a seat somewhere else on the bus. But she marched to the backseat, picked up his satchel, handed it to him, and sat down. The bus was quiet again. Everyone turned to see what Johnny would do or say. With a smile on her face, Jessie whispered, out loud, "Looks like you fell out of bed and hit your head." With a big smile, she said, "Howdy, I'm Jessie Mae, wishing you a happy day!"

I liked Jessie because she had a way of saying things

that kept me laughing on the outside and smiling on the inside, whenever it was just the two of us. But, at recess time, she kept to herself. If I was playing with Penny or Sarah, she would sneak a look at us, as she bounced her ball on the sidewalk. When I talked to Mama about it, she reminded me of my first days in an integrated school. As the months rolled along, Jessie Mae, Penny, and I became best friends.

Family Crisis

It was about a week before the end of the school year when, at dinner one day, Mama sent into orbit the fun-packed summer plans Jessie Mae, Penny and I had giggled and fussed over—in a good way, since becoming best friends.

At first, I thought it was the start of one of her stories. Mama crossed her arms, shrugged her shoulders, slowly relaxed them, then let out a long sigh and said, "I have glad news mixed with sad news." Uh, Uh, I thought to myself. This does not sound good.

"We got the news last month that Papa and Grandma Sally will need help at pea-picking time this summer. Your Daddy and Uncle Ben will drive us to Georgia at the end of the month," she said.

I looked at Elsie. She was slumped down in her chair sniffing and near tears. In a loud voice, she said, "I don't want to go back to Georgia! I miss Papa and Grandma Sally and other family, but I like Columbus, especially my school. Here, I can have friends—black and white. We can laugh and talk together, ride the city bus together, sit down and eat hamburgers at the White Castle together. I feel freer here than in Georgia. I would never have been allowed to do such things in

Georgia. But best of all, I have a nice part-time summer job. Now, I have to give it up!"

Mama said quietly, "You will be staying with Sadie and Ben until we get back. I'm sorry to spring this on you like this, but we decided to finalize things before telling you kids the plan. Ben bought a new station wagon, and he and your Daddy will drive us down and pick us up later at the end of pea-picking time."

Elsie jumped up from the table, ran to Mama—hugging her while laughing and crying at the same time.

Travel day was just a day away. I had said goodbye to my best friends, our bags were packed, including Mama's survival bag, boxes of presents for Papa and Grandma Sally, special things to keep us kids busy, and the shoeboxes ready for Mama to finish filling the next morning with food and drinks—our restaurant on wheels, I thought to myself.

Uncle Ben had come over to pick up some of our suitcases and boxes to pack in his station wagon that night. The front room, where they were talking, was next to the room where Elsie and I slept. Hearing their voices, I could not help but listen in and knew right away, the drive back to Georgia was not going to be a fun one.

Uncle Ben began:

You know, James, going through Tennessee will slow us down a bit. It's just like going through Mississippi.

Yeah, I know, Ben. The map you bought should help.

I hear they've completed a new four lane highway through there, which means driving will be a little easier.

That'll be a blessing, James. But our obeying the speed limit don't matter to 'em. We could be crawling through like a snail and still get stopped for speeding.

And, get talked down to like we're children or criminals! I'll never forget the time my brother Clarence and I drove down to Arkansas in his new car and got stopped by a state trooper....

"Where ya get this new car, boy?" the trooper said in an unfriendly voice.

"What did I do wrong, Sir?" Clarence had asked nicely.

"You trying to get uppity with me, boy?"

"No," Clarence said. "But what's my violation?"

With a smirk on his face, the trooper said, "Failing to yield."

"Yield to what?" Clarence asked, taking out his ID. Ignoring him, the trooper started writing the ticket. He paused, looked around and pointed to an old 'Yield to Cattle Crossing' sign that no one had bothered to remove, once the highway was completed.

I just shook my head, James. They know they have a pass, by the powers that be, to do whatever they want to us, because of our color.

When Clarence showed him his ID, that trooper's face turned beet red. He tore the ticket from his pad, crumbled it up and said, "Just let this be a warning!"

"What happened, Ben, to make him change his mind?"

"Maybe Clarence's new job in Washington, D.C. He never mentioned the incident again."

"Well, James," said Uncle Ben. "Seeing we need to get on the road before the rooster crows in the morning, I'm gonna mosey out of here and pack as much as I can in the station wagon. By the way, I've marked the places to stop for gas that have fairly decent toilets for us to use," he said. See ya in the morning."

After Uncle Ben left, I wanted to draw, but my mind and the lump in my chest kept bumping into each other.

I felt a hand gently shaking me awake. When did I fall asleep? I thought, turning over to take another little snooze, while Mama left to wake up Rickey and Ray-Jay.

My eyes were barely open, as Uncle Ben guided the station wagon onto the road, and we began the journey back to Georgia.

Back Home in Georgia

After the hugs, kisses, and tears, we all stood on the porch waving goodbye to Daddy and Uncle Ben after only a day's rest. They had two days to get back to their jobs.

Trailing Mama back into the house, we sat down to rest from the long trip. It wasn't long before Ray-Jay was asleep, curled up close to Grandma Sally. Papa John, in his big wide chair, patted a place for Rickey to come sit. Mama and I took the swing on the back porch to relax. Mama looked out over the big backyard and said, as if to herself, "My, oh, my. Being here takes me back many years."

"How many years, Mama?" I asked. "Was I born?"

"Before and after you were born," she said. "I was thinking about the time, when you were knee-high to a duck, my brother Tripe and I would come home in the summer to join other family members to help pick rows and rows of purple hull peas. There were always three groups—pickers, shellers, and cooks. Starting at daybreak, the pickers would make their way to the fields, following each other into narrow, dirt tracks between the rows of peas, while the shellers set up chairs, fans, ice water, and large baskets to receive the freshly picked peas. The cooks prepared enough food to keep everybody happy. Once the shelling got underway, the shellers shared health remedies, bits and pieces of gossip, and other happenings around the farms. After two rounds, they switched places—the shellers became the pickers."

Now things have changed. Papa John and Grandma Sally are no longer able to work the fields, and grownup children, unavailable for one reason or the other, had to call on friends and neighbors to help by offering them a share in the crop.

"How old were you when you started picking peas?" I asked Mama.

"At age ten, each grandchild was taught the art of pea picking. It was not easy. Purple hull peas grow on low vines, which meant we had to bend low or crawl on our knees to pull only pods with firm peas inside," she said.

"One year, when Mama let me go with her to take water to the pickers, Tripe was teasing his friend George he would be the first to fill his pan before noon. Kids only picked until noon. I watched the sun beat down on Tripe's head until sweat ran down his neck, while stinging gnats lay in wait for a bite. Tripe reached into the vines, searching between the heart-shape leaves to find the pea pods. He pinched them off and dropped them into his basket, then stopped to swat insects or wipe sweat out of his eyes with his shirt sleeves. Every time Tripe looked into his basket and then at the long rows ahead, he let out a long sigh. I was happy my tenth birthday was two years away. Up until he went off to College, Tripe always managed to come down with some type of aliment around pea-picking time. Sometimes he got away with it, but not often."

Hearing Ray-Jay's hungry cry ended Mama's story.

That evening at dinner, Mama said we had two more days of play time before pea-picking. Until then, Papa John took us kids on rides around the farm in his hay wagon, while Grandma Sally baked all kinds of goodies to please our tummies.

The night before pea picking, Rickey had strutted around like he was King of the Mountain, teasing me because I was not old enough to go pea picking with the grown-ups. To protect him from the hot sun and the bugs, Grandma Sally gave him a large bag. In it were overalls, a long sleeve shirt, and a lopsided straw hat. When Rickey tried them on, Grandma Sally said in a quiet voice, "Those belonged to your Uncle Tripe when he was ten. Come here boy, let me hug you. You look so much like him." Tears rose in her eyes, as Rickey hugged her back.

When I got up the next morning, the sun was just peeking over the little hill out back. I stood at the window watching the first group of pickers make their way down the long path to the field. Rickey, along with other kids, ten or older, were running ahead of the grown-ups, excited about their new adventure.

Later that morning, with my pad and pencil, I went looking for a place that would give me shade from the hot sun, while Ray-Jay chased a stray baby chick around the barnyard until the mother hen chased him away.

I finally settled myself under a nearby weeping willow tree, out of sight of Mama and the others setting up for shelling, and was about to start drawing, when I overheard Uncle George say, "That girl Kandi is gonna be a real artist one day."

I smiled inside and out until my great Uncle Ned chimed in, "Well, I think she should spend more time playing with other *chilluns* instead of squiggling all the time. That girl is skittish of her own shadow."

From inside the kitchen, I heard the clanging of pots and pans, then, Grandma Sally's voice. Looking around the tree, I saw her standing in the doorway, one hand in the pocket of her big, colorful bib apron, a large spoon in the other, and shiny beads of sweat trickling down her face. "Ned Blanton!" she said loudly.

Mama told us that when Grandma Sally called you by your first and last name in the same breath, it meant you had troubled her mind in some way. All shelling and talking stopped. Looking at her brother, she said, "Some gifts are in need of a special kinda handling before unwrapping, so as not to damage what's precious inside." Pausing, she took a handkerchief from her pocket, dabbed her face dry and continued, in a softer voice, "It's that way with people sometimes, especially some children. Now you hush up about Kandi." Shaking her head, she returned to the kitchen, leaving the pea-shelling folks taking side glances at Uncle Ned—happy it was not one of them who had troubled Grandma Sally's mind.

Looking around, Papa John broke the silence saying, "There *is* something special about Kandi." Then, eyeballing Uncle Ned, he said, "Miz Loree Johnson said those very words at the church supper last year." Heads nodded in agreement, until Uncle Ned, in an effort to improve his wilted ego, led the porch talk to the best dishes at the last church supper, and how good Miz Johnson looked for her age.

Now, just about everybody in Granville, Georgia had respect for Miz Johnson, especially Papa John. She was the one responsible for his son becoming the success he turned out to be.

Easing back in his chair, his southern drawl reminding me of mine a few years back, he said, "We just couldn't understand why Clyde hated school so much. That boy could usually figure out just about anything he put his mind to, even when young'uns his own age and even some of us old folks couldn't—as long as it didn't have to do with writing something. Well, one day, Miz Johnson sent a note home by Clyde that she needed to talk to Sally and me. We went in the next day, wondering what in the world Clyde had done."

"Please come in and have a seat, Mr. and Mrs. Smith,' she said kindly. Right away, she asked if we had ever had Clyde's eyes checked. We hadn't, 'cause he had never let on to us that he couldn't see, and even if he had, we had little money to get to Atlanta and even less money to see the eye doctor. Well, it turned out, according to Miz Johnson, a new white eye doctor had moved into town and word was, he took Negro patients. After a few bake sales and other projects, sponsored by Miz Johnson and the PTA, we got help in getting glasses for Clyde. In no time at all, Clyde could hardly wait to get to school! That Miz Johnson is a smart lady. She finished high school, went to college, got a degree, when life was pretty much laid out for us by other folks. Miz Johnson laid out her own way. It was hard but she did it!"

The group grew quiet again, like they were meditating on what Papa John had said. Then, from the kitchen, Grandma Sally started humming, *Amazing Grace*—picked up by the porch group, and the hymn singing was on!

Settling myself under the tree with my pad, it wasn't long before my imagination traveled from my head, right smack into my fingers, and before I knew it, a likeness of Miz Johnson started to appear on my pad. I was anxious for the summer to be over so I could get back to my friends, especially Penny and Jessie.

When the first crew returned from the fields for lunch, Rickey had the look of a withered cucumber. Weighed down with his half-full pan of peas, unlike the overflowing pans of some of the other kids, Rickey's face lit up like a candle when Grandma Sally said kids only picked for a half day. That evening, as the sun slowly fell behind the horizon, so did Rickey's enthusiasm for pea picking.

The weeks flew by quickly, and before too long Uncle Ben and Daddy returned, and after a day's rest, we were on the road, headed home. The word 'home' tickled my insides and put a smile on my face.

"Daddy," I said bouncing about on my seat, after reading the sign, *Columbus City Limits*. "I can hardly wait to get home and see Penny and Jessie Mae. Do you think..."

Before I could finish, Daddy turned around, and the look on his face erased the happiness I was feeling. I looked at Mama, and knew, as she patted my hand that she knew what Daddy was about to say.

"The day after Ben and I returned from Georgia," he said. "I saw Penny's mom walking toward the old barn.

"*Hi, James*, she said, waving me toward her. I could tell something was out of kilter. *How did you leave Fannie and the kids—and her parents?*

"Noticing her wet eyes, I said, *A bit sad, especially Kandi. She's anxious to...*

"*You and your family have been good neighbors since you moved here*, she blurted out. *Oh, I'm so sorry to cut you off. I have such devastating news!*

"*Go on*, I said, now really worried.

"Taking a deep breath, she said, *It has been good seeing our friendship grow—especially between the children. As you know, Jack is a southerner, but he doesn't harbor ill will toward Negroes because the north won the Civil War.* Smiling shyly, she said, *but he has family members who do, and that's what making our* move to Texas heartbreaking. Penny cried her eyes out when we told them the news. Seth doesn't show his feelings easily, but I know he will miss Rickey.

"Oh my gosh! I said. *What in the world happened?*

"Jack's parents were in a bad car wreck several weeks ago. His father died after two days; his mother hung on until last month—bringing to the forefront, a situation—dealing with his sister, that left Jack in charge of the family's estate."

When Daddy got to the part about Penny's family moving, my ears shut out the rest of his words and tears filled my eyes, washing away my excitement. Mama held me close, but it did not take away the sadness that spread inside me. I drew pictures for about a week to help me get through missing them so much.

Instead of having fun sharing with Penny and Jessie Mae page after page of drawings of my encounters with a pesky mother hen and her chicks, watching cute little piglets and calves suckle, my drawing board stared back at me as blank as those of my feelings, with each sheet I tore away.

By the time school started, I still missed Penny, but the news from Daddy that we would be moving to Texas in six months snatched me back to that mixed-emotions thing—being happy and sad at the same time. Now, Jessie Mae would be missing me like I missed Penny.

Jessie Mae was not at the bus stop the first two days

of school. It was day two and Mr. Polk couldn't wait any longer. As the bus pulled away, I prayed she would come running from around the corner, but she didn't.

Soon, we were at school. In the classroom, I hung my coat in the coat room and was on my way to my desk when I realized the classroom was really quiet, except for a few whispers. Even Tye Jones, who liked teasing everybody first thing, was sitting quietly at his desk, as though looking for something. Our teacher, Mrs. Dawson, was walking around the classroom, listening and chatting with us, as she usually did before the bell rang to start the day.

When Mrs. Dawson called the roll, she skipped Jessie Mae's name. I wonder if she knows why Jessie Mae is not at school, I thought to myself. When she finished, she said, "Boys and girls, I know some of you are concerned about Jessie Mae and maybe why she has not been in class. Today, I learned it is a family matter."

My stomach did a somersault. I stared at Mrs. Dawson. Are her eyes watery? Do I hear sadness in her voice? Under my breath, I whispered, "What family matter?" Jessie Mae loved talking about her family, especially her sister, Louise, who still lived in Alabama with her grandmother. Maybe something happened to her, I thought.

We soon moved into our classroom activities. Everything was in slow motion for me, until it was time to go to art. Once there, I immediately opened my portfolio and began work on "Penny's Old Barn", the title of my show-piece for next week's art show. I was so deep in thought, I didn't realize the art teacher, Miss Knight, was standing close by looking at my work.

"Kandi," she said, coming closer. "What a magnificent-looking barn! Is there a story behind it?"

I wanted to say how afraid of the old barn I was when I first saw it, and how, after Penny and her family moved away, I got over my fear, when it helped me solve a mystery. But instead, I relived it, as my hand began to move over my pad:

Light snow was falling the Saturday morning we heard a knock at our backdoor. It was Mr. Stewart from up the street. "Good morning, Jack," I heard Daddy say. Come in."

"Oh, no," Mr. Stewart said. "Is Rickey here?" he asked. I need to ask him a question.

Spacing his words out, Daddy said slowly, "Maybe you need to come in and tell me what this is about." Mr. Stewart stepped inside the room. "Did Rickey do something wrong?"

"Well," he said, "Yesterday, Rickey and the Johnston boy stopped by to play with my nephew who was visiting for the day. I help my sister out with him, since his daddy died. I was cleaning my old gun and they wanted to watch me. I let them, telling them how nobody should fool around with a gun if they didn't know how to use it, especially them. When they left to play outside, I put the gun on a high shelf and went about my day, in and outside. This morning it was missing. My nephew said Rickey took it, and the other

just started crying that it wasn't him. I'm not putting all the blame on Rickey. I just want to hear his side of the story.

I could see Daddy was very upset. He called Rickey, and I overheard him, almost in tears, say he didn't take the gun. I felt sorry for Rickey and left to go outside to catch some of the falling snow for homemade ice cream. That's when I saw shoeprints leading to the old barn. For some reason, I don't know today why, it was like the barn was speaking to me, leading me inside, even though I was scared to go in by myself. I followed the tracks to the barn door. It was not latched. Peeking in, at first, the light from the loft's window was enough to see some of the places Penny and I had played. There were big cabinets with closed doors and small cabinets with no doors. I stepped further inside, stopped and looked around. From where I stood, I saw something by itself on an open shelf. I walked slowly over to it. It was a gun! I ran back and told Daddy. It turned out to be Mr. Stewart's gun.

The short of this sad story was that Rickey took the gun on a dare. When they heard Mr. Stewart coming back, Rickey, scared, hid it under his jacket, thinking, he said later, to put it back the next day. My brother was in deep trouble with Daddy and Mama for a long time.

Miss Knight's, "Five minutes to clean-up," startled me back from the memories of the time I was afraid of the old barn.

I looked down at my drawing, and, to my surprise, saw changes I had made during the class that would show my old friend in a new way. I could hardly wait to put the finishing touches on it at the next class.

During the art class, my mind strayed from Jessie Mae, but returning to the classroom started things up all over again. When the bell to dismiss sounded, I could hardly wait to get home.

A week rolled around before I could talk myself into asking Miss Dawson about Jessie Mae.

"I'm sorry Kandi, I know you miss Jessie Mae, but we'll just have to wait and see if and when she returns to school."

The very next day, I was excited to see Jessie Mae on the playground. I wondered why she wasn't on the bus, but I didn't care about that. "Jessie Mae! You're back!" I said running to her. "Where have you been?

I knew something was wrong when Jessie Mae didn't say anything right away. She looked at me, then turned her face away. Slowly she turned around. Her eyes filled with tears, she said, "My sister Louise is missing down in Alabama, and we have to move back to help take care of my Grandmama. We leave tomorrow.

"Wha...what... hap...happened?" I stuttered.

"I can't talk about it, Kandi," she said, so softly I could hardly make out her words. My mama is inside telling my teacher we are moving. She let me come with her to say goodbye to her...and you. Biting her lips down hard, as if to keep the tears away, they rolled down her face, anyway. I wanted to say something, but knew I would have a hard time getting my words out, because I was so nervous. The bell rang. I hugged her, then ran to get in line.

When school was out, I rushed to get on the bus and get home to free my backed-up tears. "Mama! Mama! I said, feeling the tears sliding down my face. "Jessie Mae is leaving for Alabama tomorrow."

Burying my head in her opened arms, she said, "I know, honey. I know. It is a sad story. I saw Mrs. Monroe last week at the bus line, and she shared a few things with me about it."

Hearing those words, I knew whatever Mrs. Monroe shared would be on the shelf for a while. But I did find out bits and pieces on the rides to and from school and the playground. It was like a big puzzle with missing pieces that everybody was looking for but couldn't find. The bits and pieces went something like this:

A cab driver came to her grandmama's house at 10:00 o'clock one night and told her that her daughter, Vivian, had sent him to get Louise because things had backed up at work, and she needed Louise to come to the restaurant to help her. At first, her grandmama said it was getting too late, but then remembered that Vivian had taken Louise with her a few times to make a little extra money as a dishwasher, so she let her go. Louise had not been seen since, and just about everybody who lived across the other side of the train tracks was looking for her.

After a few weeks, the bits and pieces faded out, replaced by calls for prayers by the churches and the NAACP. I prayed every night that Louise would be found, so Jessie Mae and her family could come back to Columbus.

I knew Mama worried about me when I stopped drawing. I was moping around one day when she asked, "Kandi, would you like to take music lessons? Mrs. Brown, the musician at church, thinks you might like to join a new group she's starting."

I wonder where she got that idea, I said to myself. Then I remembered playing around on the piano keys before one of our youth choir rehearsals. Feeling I wasn't alone, I turned around to see her standing in the door listening. She asked, "Kandi. Have you had piano lessons before?"

I started to shake my head no, but remembered Mama said I should always use my voice when only a *yes* or *no* answer was necessary. "No—no ma'am," I said. Then to my surprise, I said without stuttering, "We don't have a piano."

"Well, you picked out a lot of friendly-sounding notes that got along with each other," she said smiling. "If you can come to choir rehearsal 30 minutes early, I'll introduce you formally to the piano, and we'll go from there. I'll call your Mom." Some kind of switch turned on inside me, making me feel happy all over!

A few weeks later, Daddy surprised us with the news that his boss was looking for someone to take an old standup piano off his hands, and it was free of charge to anyone who could pick it up before the end of the week. Looking at me smiling, he said, "Anybody around here interested in having a piano?"

"Yes, Daddy, but where would it go?"

"Don't you worry about that. By some hook or crook, we'll find a place for it."

The next day, Daddy and Uncle Ben sat in a moving truck deciding how to get the piano into our small house. With the help of Mr. Pepper and his son from across the street, and, after much huffing and puffing and moaning and groaning, they were finally able to get it in the front door and into our front room. It wasn't long before Mama said I took to the piano like a duck to water.

The piano brought a new interest into my life and opened the door to others.

Fourth grade composition was one of the *others*. My visit to the public library to get my library card was another. Both helping to heal the wounds after my friends, Jessie Mae and Penny moved away.

Reckoning with a Bully

It was near the end of fourth grade that I had a run-in with Johnny Jackson.

We had art that day, and I was happy as a lark because I was not only bringing home my art portfolio to share with my family, but Rickey and I now walked to Aunt Sadie's after school. She and Uncle Ben had moved into a nice house close by. When Elsie got the part-time job, Aunt Sadie dropped by. "Fannie," she said, kind of bossy, "Rickey and Kandi are too young to be home alone after school. So, when you pick up Ray-Jay, you can pick them up, too." Being the older sister, Mama let Aunt Sadie boss her around, but in a good way.

At first, walking to Aunt Sadie's was kind of scary for me, because there was always a bunch of kids, especially some of the boys, running around teasing others. Nobody bothered me when Rickey was around, but it was Wednesday, and his Boy Scout meeting was after school. I was a little nervous walking alone, but tried not to let on.

"Hi, Kandi," said a voice behind me. It was Annie Maude, a friend of Elsie's. She was in the eighth grade and had become friends with Elsie last summer, when she spent the summer with her Aunt Lillie, who lived just two doors from us.

"Hi, I said, feeling safer with her catching up to walk with me, especially when I saw Johnny Jackson running in and out of groups. I guess he's been kicked off the bus again, I thought. It had rained earlier that morning, and he was jumping in some of the puddles, splashing water around. I held tightly to my books and portfolio.

"Hey, Kandi," said Johnny running up fast and stopping short in front of us—like he was putting on brakes. "Where's your slow-talking friend, Jessie Mae?" he asked, mimicking a southern drawl. I didn't say anything. I kept close to Annie Maude and two of her friends who had caught up with us. We started walking away.

Johnny ran up again and mimicked, "What kinda candy bar are you, Kandi? A Hershey? A Butternut? A Snicker? Some kids thought that was funny and snickered.

Annie Maude said, "Leave Kandi alone, Johnny. Go pick on someone who's not scared of you." He then grabbed my portfolio. A favorite drawing slipped out. He tried to snatch it, but it floated out of his reach and landed in a nearby puddle. I watched as the colors turned into a blur. I picked up my portfolio and shoved my ruined drawing in it. Then came the chant, "Scaredy cat, scaredy cat." That was followed by others saying, "Get him, Kandi, Get him, Kandi." I turned around and stopped. My eyes met Dylan's, Johnny's

48

friend. He was not chanting, but looking at me with eyes that seemed to say, "I'm sorry."

A strange feeling rose from somewhere deep inside me. With tears filling my eyes, I slowly walked away, scared and trembling. Suddenly, out of nowhere, my books and portfolio were flying in the air; I was feeling disconnected in some way. With my eyes closed, I sailed into Johnny, my arms flinging, my hands thrashing wherever they might, but I didn't care. I don't know what happened to Johnny. When I came to myself, kids were laughing and shouting, "Kandi won!" Annie Maude and her friends hugged me and said, "You should've seen him running away, Kandi. I bet he won't mess with you again."

At the dinner table that night, I was cheered on by my family, after listening to the details from Rickey's second-hand account that he'd heard from a friend. Not wanting to re-live it, I sat in silence. After everyone left the table except for Mama, she looked at me, smiled, shook her head and said, "Kandi, I'm happy you stood up for yourself today." She paused, took my hands and said, "While physical fighting is usually not a good thing, unless your life is in danger, you learned something about yourself today. You probably won't know the how and what of it right away, but you will in time. That's when you will recall with clarity and understanding today's delayed revelation."

That night, I couldn't fall asleep. My mind played back the whole day over and over. I thought about Mama's words, especially the revelation thing. I got up and checked the word in the dictionary to see if I could understand Mama's words better. I didn't, so I got back in bed and counted sheep until sleep slipped in without my knowing it.

On the Road Again?

About a month before the end of the school year Daddy made what was, to us, two earth-shaking announcements: He had bought a car, and the move to Tennessee was now changed to Hillsborough, Texas. We were all excited about the new car.

Rickey asked, "Is it a big or little car, Daddy?"

Daddy winked at Mama and said, "Let's look and see." What a ruckus we made following Daddy and Mama outside to see the shiny, blue station wagon parked in front of our house.

Elsie forgot her daily nagging about the moving date and being a senior in September; I forgot about thinking Penny and I would run to meet each other on a street in Texas; Rickey and Ray-Jay, in the right-now, were having fun jumping around in the backseat. Mama, in the front seat, was smiling, touching the soft leather seats, while Elsie and I sat prim and proper in the middle seat, anxious for Daddy to power up the engine for our first ride!

A few weeks later, after a trip to Texas, Daddy showed us a picture of a nice-looking house. It was long, with a large front yard that had little bushes around it. I liked the big window on the front and the long walkway that led to the front door. He said it was a ranch with lots of room, like the one on Parker Street. We all glanced at it, trying not to remember that awful day, until Daddy whispered out loud, "I've signed with the bank. It's ours. No one can take it away!" What a commotion Elsie, Rickey and I made, shouting and jumping all over the place. Ray-Jay joined in, not really understanding why we were so excited. Running to them with hugs and kisses, we nearly knocked Mama and Daddy over.

It was Saturday morning, a few weeks later, when we learned about the glitch in the move to Texas. Elsie was about to get into her woe-is-me complaint about how moving to Texas meant returning to the indignities of segregation. That was when Daddy cleared his throat and said, "Yesterday, I learned our move to Texas will be delayed five to six months."

"Five to six months!" Elsie let out, in a high-pitched voice. "Daddy, that means I will be a senior half-time here and half-time in Texas."

"I know, honey, but things are in place, and it's too late to unravel them now. I can't turn down this promotion, and there are new voices speaking out against Jim Crow laws."

Mama said, "Hmm, we're in a pickle. Will this end with sweet pickle relish, dill pickle relish, or just swallowing the whole pickle?" Mama had a way of using words to make us "ponder." This was one of them.

I didn't feel happy about leaving Columbus, either. Just thinking about having to ride on the back of the bus or having to drink water from the "Colored" drinking fountain made me sad. I got my drawing paper and pencil set to put my feelings on paper.

A few weeks later, Aunt Sadie invited us over for Sunday dinner. Afterwards, Rickey and Ray-Jay played in the backyard until both came back and fell asleep on the davenport in what Aunt Sadie called the family room. Elsie eased into a chair next to Mama. No one said anything.

From the nearby living room, where I sat reading, I heard Aunt Sadie say, "Now, Fannie, you and James wouldn't have to worry about Elsie. We enjoyed having her here when you and the other kids left to help with the purple hull pea harvest. You know we have plenty room. Staying here, she can graduate with her classmates at East High School, where she'll get a much better education than down south.

Looking at Elsie, Uncle Ben said, "Graduating from high school here may put you on the fast track at one of the smaller colleges, or even OSU, if your grades are good enough."

Mama and Daddy nodded their heads all which ways—mostly listening to Aunt Sadie and Uncle Ben, with a few grunts here and there.

Elsie didn't say much at first, but when there was a long pause in the conversation, she threw questions at them like darts at a dartboard.

It wasn't long before it was time to leave. On our

way home, Mama said, "I wonder what kind of pickle juice we're going to get from the pickle we're in?"

To our surprise, Rickey said, "Sweet and Sour."

The summer went by quickly. I knew the new-found freedoms we had grown used to in Columbus would be over in Texas. I still thought about Louise, wondering if she was ever found, and how much Jessie Mae had changed since the last time I saw her.

Starting school in September was a letdown for all of us because of the move. I was in fifth grade and my teacher was Mrs. Fisher. I knew I would miss Mrs. Dawson's way of putting me at ease, whenever my nervousness and stuttering got in the way of my learning a new skill.

Mama left her job, just as the chilling, north winds began shaking loose the colorful autumn leaves that decorated wherever they landed. Also, there were the smooth, brown buckeyes we collected for art projects, when we weren't having fun crushing them under our stomping feet—much to the aggravation of lawn mower pushers.

We knew the move was real the day the moving van people showed up, packed most of our belongings and drove away, leaving us with suitcases and boxes filled with things we would need on the train, including Mama's survival bag.

The next week, the Kane family, except Elsie, boarded a train to Waco, Texas, for the first leg of the trip to Hillsborough. Daddy had driven down earlier to leave the station wagon, returning by bus to Columbus to make our journey easier, as southern hotels and restaurants did not accommodate Negro customers.

Leaving was harder than we all thought, especially for Elsie. Our last night in Columbus was with Uncle Ben and Aunt Sadie. Early the next morning, Elsie put on a smiling face; she didn't know I heard her muffled cries during the night.

After the hugs, tears, and kisses, we squeezed ourselves inside Uncle Ben's station wagon. He was taking us to the train station. As we got on the road, I looked back and saw Aunt Sadie and Elsie standing on the porch. Aunt Sadie had her arm around Elsie, both were waving until they disappeared out of sight. Mama began humming a new little tune.

Starting Over—Again!

The train ride from Ohio to Texas was very different from the one from Georgia to Ohio. When we changed trains, it was like our lives were in reverse. I was beginning to feel nervous and a little scared about moving so far away where we had no family or friends.

The most significant thing about this train ride was it took almost three days to get to the train station in Waco, which was about 30 minutes from Hillsborough.

Once we got ourselves and our belongings off the train, a tall man walked up to us and, in a loud, friendly voice, said, "Howdy yall." Tipping his hat to Mama, he said, "Welcome, to Texas, Ma'am. "I bet you all are worn out from the long train ride." Winking   at us kids, he said, "Come on, you cowhands, let's saddle up and get on down the road. Old Susie is raring to go."

"Thanks for picking us up, Clyde," Daddy said, in a tired voice. With Mr. Clyde's help, we gathered our belongings and followed him to a faded green station wagon. Once everybody was settled in, Mr. Clyde headed old Susie to our new home.

It was late in the evening when we got to the house. It looked like the one in the picture Daddy showed us, except Daddy's station wagon was parked in the driveway under something that looked like a shed. We learned later that it was called a carport.

Mr. Clyde helped us to get all our belongings inside, and stayed to help Daddy put up the beds so we would have a place to sleep. The next few days we all were busy setting up our new home. Once everything was in place, we still had empty spaces. Mama laughed and said, "Our house in Columbus could easily set into this house, with room to spare. I guess I'll have to go furniture shopping soon."

The next week Mama took us to register at school. It was Daddy's day off, and he stayed home with Ray-Jay; registration for the primary students was the following week. When we arrived, we were shocked to see an old, three-story, red brick building that we later learned went from first to twelfth grade. The primary grades were on the first floor, middle grades, the second, and high school, the third floor.

Mr. Washington, the principal, welcomed us into his office, inviting Mama to take a seat, and leading Rickey and I to another room with a window, tables, chairs, and books. Leaving the door open, and returning to sit at his desk, he said to Mama, "Rickey's and Kandi's school records from Ohio arrived last week. We like our new parents to come in and sign the enrollment papers. It gives the school and parents a chance to greet and meet, in the event there are concerns or questions."

Mama took the papers, and handed them back to him after signing them.

"We are pleased to have new families move into our little town," he said, noticing that Mama was not talking much.

Mama said, "I was told I could get teacher assignment cards today."

Clearing his throat, Mr. Washington said, "I know, coming from a big city in the north, 'separate, but equal' schools boggles the mind. Construction of our new building is nearly complete, but things are still not equal. Even though space is a problem, Mrs. Kane, we have good teachers here at Peabody, dedicated to teaching our children the 3Rs and more, despite the inequality heaped on us by those who hold the purse strings and the power; a better day is on the horizon".

I knew Mama had something to say on the matter, and she did.

"Yes, Mr. Washington. I heard about that better day coming when I was growing up in Georgia. I'm not blaming you, and, though we are concerned about the old school building, we will adjust and find ways to live with it, until the new school is complete."

Uh, uh, I said to myself. From the tone of her voice, the principal was about to get a talking to, whether he wanted it or not.

"The stark inequality," she began, "is how physically close boundary lines can be between black and white neighborhoods, but yet, so far apart ideologically. Across the street from our home is a little knoll that slopes down to a ditch. Just over that knoll is a large piece of land on which there are two schools for whites: elementary, and a high school a little further down. My children, as well as other children on the other side of the ditch, pass by those schools every day, walk a quarter mile through a field, and cross a busy, dangerous highway just to get to one 3-story school—not a school with rolling green grass nor ample play space and playground equipment for them to enjoy before, during, or after school."

Mama stood up to leave, beckoning us to follow her. At the door she said, "It was nice meeting you, Mr. Washington, and please don't feel my words, though sharp, are for you, but anger at an evil system here in the south that has been allowed to continue in our country year after year and generation after generation. We look forward to completion of the new school." Leaving the room, I looked back at Mr. Washington. He had a faint smile on his face.

Now, a fifth grader, I became more aware of the boundaries that separated black and white people. Not only in schools, but just about everywhere in our lives—none helped me feel good about why we moved.

When we lived under segregation in the south, I was excited about school, and was sad when we left. That sadness followed me into Fulton Elementary school in Columbus where, at first, I had mixed emotions as a second grader. Being older, my feelings now were more of anger than sadness.

It wasn't long before there was excited chatter at home, at school, and the neighborhood that the new school was finally complete! The favorite pastime of just about everybody in the community was either riding or walking by the site just to gaze at the long, one story building, with its ample space for the football team to practice, and a playground area for all grades to use at different times when school was in session.

The move from the old, worn-down, building that had been school to many generations of black children, addressed an era of orchestrated neglect by those who held the power to do so. The textbook budget farce, according to complaints by black educators, was a case in point—when new editions of textbooks were issued in the white schools, the old editions were shipped to the black schools.

Open House was attended by just about everybody in our community. There were a lot of oohs and aahs, and a feeling maybe things would get better for us—at least we had a new school building with a nice auditorium that served as a gym and lunchroom. The new library was much larger.

One Saturday, when Rickey and I were walking to school to a basketball game, we heard church music close by. Checking it out, we discovered a church beyond a bunch of trees we hadn't noticed before. I talked Mama into a visit the next Sunday; it was Youth Sunday, and the young people were in charge of the service. I was surprised when I saw the familiar face of our paper carrier; he was two grades ahead of me. When he gave a prayer, I found myself liking his strong voice, but it was the youth choir I liked best. Their swaying and clapping with the fast, high-spirited songs rocked the church!

On the way home, Mama said, "I enjoyed the service today. We'll have to come for a regular service."

We did, and, after a few more visits with the rest of the family, we became members. I was a candidate for baptism, and after going through a preparation period with other kids my age, we were baptized one Sunday evening. The experience was one that left an indelible mark on my Christian journey into adulthood. Daddy later became a deacon and Mama a Sunday school teacher.

Our first year in Texas crawled by like a turtle with arthritis in every joint. It was taking forever before Elsie's graduation day. We talked on the phone and sent cards and letters to each other, but that made me want to see her more. Once I got more involved with school and school activities, it wasn't long before the Texas winter, unlike the cold, snowy, winter in Columbus, had morphed into spring, and weeks later, we were on our way to Columbus for Elsie's graduation.

"Lordy, me," said Aunt Sadie, "It's good to see y'all. I think I need to get bricks for your heads, you growing up so fast! The next evening, we piled into Uncle Ben's station wagon, headed to East High School, proud to see Elsie get her diploma.

On our way home, Elsie said, "Mama, Miss Jackson asked if I would like to work in the store fulltime and I said I would."

"But Elsie," I said, "you don't want to come home with us? It's like a real house you see in magazines." I was near tears, but I held them back.

"What about college, Elsie?" Daddy said, trying not to push her panic button. "We want you to come home with us and look for a job there."

"Daddy, you know my options would be limited to menial jobs and you know why. I like my job here very much. One day, when we were really busy in the store, Miss Jackson said, 'Elsie I've been watching you at work, pleased with the ease and confidence in which you handle yourself with customers—some get quite testy, from time to time. There are college degrees in this line of work, and if you decide on a school in Columbus, you could continue your work here in the summer as you prepare for college.'

"Please, Mama and Daddy. Aunt Sadie and Uncle Ben said I can continue to stay with them, if it's okay with you."

At first, Mama and Daddy were undecided about allowing Elsie to stay, but in the end, Aunt Sadie won out—again!

Our short visit to Columbus was over, and we were back in Texas where the temperature sometimes reached a hundred degrees. Daddy bought fans to cool the house until our bodies adjusted to the heat. I had met a few friends at school, but it was too hot to visit. There was a public park with a swimming pool, but we couldn't use it because of the Jim Crow laws. Besides, most of the kids my age, and some younger, had to chop and later pick cotton with their families to have money for the winter months. Our school helped by delaying the start of school until after harvest time.

One day, Mama came home excited.

"Guess what, Kandi?" she said, after Mrs. Rowe, a lady from church, drove away. "I found a music teacher for you; she lives just a block away."

I liked the idea because taking lessons and practicing would help fill my time, since my drawing pad remained out of sight. I wanted to go to the public library to check out books but, again, was not allowed because of those stupid laws. After helping Mama put away the groceries, she handed me a piece of paper with the day, time, address, and the name of my new music teacher, Miss Nancy Brock. I started lessons the next week.

Rickey spent most of his free time playing with his new friends, Carl Green and Allen Jones, in a field behind our house. Ray-Jay played with his toys, when he wasn't bugging Mama or me.

Finally, school started. I was in the sixth grade, and Miss Hyson was my English teacher. I liked her right away because she reminded me of Mrs. Dawson. One day, after class, she asked me stop by her room after school. I was a little nervous about why.

"Come in, Kandi," she said, noticing I was standing outside her room. "You may sit wherever you like." I found a seat close to where she was sitting at her desk.

"Ha-have I-I done something wrong?" I asked, getting upset over my stuttering.

Smiling, she said, "No. But I've noticed, from time to time, your nervousness in class. What I'd like is for you take a deep breath and try to relax. Like this." I imitated her a few times, and was amazed that my nervousness slowly ebbed away. She handed me a card, requesting I read silently the first the four lines, then out loud:

Break, break, break,
On thy cold grey stones, O Sea!
And I would that my tongue could utter
The thoughts that arise in me.

After following her directions, she said, "You read that very well, Kandi. Now, what I'd like you to do is memorize the first four lines, and when you're ready, the rest of it. After we finish our sessions on diagramming sentences, we will begin our literary sessions, which you will introduce by reciting this Alfred Tennyson poem to the class. How do you feel about that?" she asked.

"Is that all I have to do?" She smiled and said yes. I wondered if my stuttering had something to do with what she wanted me to do. It didn't take me long to memorize the entire poem, but I was not in a hurry to recite it.

When I told Mama about it, she said, "You can practice on us as your class." I'm sure, after a while, they were looking forward to the end of it. On the weekend, they heard it morning, noon, and night.

In the meantime, I was really getting into diagraming sentences. Annie Ruth Andrews, a classmate, was a wiz at it, and I wanted to be as good at it as she was. In the end, it was composition and literature that melted my heart. Our friendly competition gave way to a lasting friendship.

A Matter of the Heart

The years flowed along—as a preteen, like a warm, soothing breeze; as a teenager, like a gust of wind taking my breath away; as a young adult, like a mist drizzling through the clouds onto my life experiences, in the wake of changes in mind, body and soul.

Our church was filled with young people, and I reluctantly settled down to being a Texan because of it. The music director asked me to be one of the pianists for the youth choir. At first, I thought it might not work out for me, but since all I had to do was play the music in front of me, as prompted by the director, I grew to like it.

To my astonishment one Sunday, when I was at the piano, there standing in the pulpit was our former paper carrier bringing the message. He glanced down and smiled at me. From that moment on, I found myself being really attentive, not only because of his deep voice, but his message was a good one, aimed at the youth. After the service, he came to the piano and said, "I really enjoyed your playing this morning, Miss Kane."

I said, "Thank you, and you don't have to call me Miss Kane. My name is K..."

"Kandi," he finished. Suddenly, there were people, young and old, surrounding him and shaking his hand: some telling him they enjoyed his message; some asking whether or not he liked the seminary he was attending. When he walked away, I do believe my heart did a little flip.

Separate, But Equal Debunked!

When I was a junior in high school, the English teacher, Miss Fisher, asked if I, along with Elroy Brown, a senior, would be interested in entering a writing contest, sponsored by the Hillsborough School Department that included all the schools—even Peabody! The guidelines included topics related to studies in the curriculum from which we could choose and develop into a composition. Elroy and I agreed to enter the contest.

When I told Mama and Daddy about it, they were excited, especially Mama, in her own funny way.

"You mean they are going to allow competition between black and white students? My! My! My! Is the world coming to an end?"

Daddy jumped in to say, "Maybe their 'separate, but equal' idea is getting another *whupping* by the NAACP."

"How in the world did that little slogan, with all the evil it stands for get touted as the best way to keep peace between black and white people," Mama said, ending with, "Oh, well."

The topic I chose was "The Circulatory System." Unable to use the public library, because of Jim Crow, I had only the resources of our school library to dig for more information. Miss Fisher said she would select books on the subject and check them out at the public library. For whatever the reason, black teachers could check out books under certain circumstances, but did not have the same privilege of unrestricted use as the white residents did. I spent several weeks getting my paper ready, reading and re-reading for errors of any kind, and writing and re-writing, as there were no typewriters available at our school. I had learned to type when I spent a summer with Aunt Sadie, but we didn't have a typewriter either. I had to handwrite the entire composition.

Several weeks later, Miss Fisher asked me to come see her after school. I was excited that it might be about my paper. It was. Her door was open, and I cleared my throat as I entered. She looked up and motioned for me to close the door. She smiled a little bit and said, "Kandi, I received your essay back."

"How did I do," I asked, feeling jittery and excited.

"Take a seat," she said, removing something from a folder on her desk "We are so proud of you and your work, Kandi. You were given an A+. Now, before you get excited, I need to share something with you that doesn't make sense to me, the principal, or anyone with common sense."

"Bu-but if I made an A+, isn't tha-that good?"

"Yes, Kandi. I read your essay and was sure it would get high marks. I called your parents and shared how proud we are of you and Elroy." Putting the paper down, and resting her head in her hand, she looked at me sorrowfully and said, "It was felt by one of the judges that you must have received help from an adult, and for that reason, even though the paper itself is A+, you would not be given full credit."

"Bu-but wh-why? Tears filled my eyes and my heart was thumping, like it sometimes did when my feelings were all over the place, and I felt itty bitty. "But Miss Fisher, I didn't get help from anyone. I wanted it to be special, not only for my mama and daddy, but for our school." There was a knock on the door. It was Mama.

Miss Fisher said, "I asked your mom to pick you up because we didn't want you to walk home after this meeting."

Mama was more than upset! She put her purse and jacket on a desk and sat down. "Thank you, Miss Fisher," she began, "for calling to explain the idiocy of a decision by an education system, based on a skewed belief that will probably affect my child and others like her, into perpetuity! That the hue of her skin, the texture of her hair, her physical features—all God given by the way—somehow stamp her as incapable of writing an essay on her own at the age of seventeen. A child with a burning desire to learn, who loved to read and write her own little stories, once she learned those skills, despite personal challenges she's in the process of overcoming, mostly on her own."

Miss Fisher was affected by Mama's words. The scene was kind of eerie. The three of us, eyes filled with tears, shared a silent moment of truth of our helplessness, not of our own making, but of those who sit in their ivory towers flaunting their power over us. Though I could not explain the how and what of it, something stirred within me, causing a different something to shift. That so-called power began to crumble that day, and in years to come, it would finally be broken and I would be free!

After dinner that evening, Mama and I shared the unusual day we had at school with Miss Fisher. Daddy, who usually measured his words in such matters, said, in a strong voice: "The time has come that we as fathers, sons, grandfathers, brothers, and uncles reclaim what was stolen from us all these many years through mechanisms designed to keep us in line through fear and unjust laws." He then excused himself from the table and left the room.

The phone rang. It was Rickey. Now a freshman at Paul Quinn College in Waco, he was a regular at home on the weekends, mostly for home-cooked meals and to do his laundry. There was a bus from Waco to Hillsborough twice a day, making it an easy way for him to come home.

"Hey Kandi," he said, when I answered the phone. "I'm catching a ride with a friend who lives just around the corner. "See ya in about an hour."

The next day was Saturday, and it was like being back in Columbus. The aroma of frying bacon floated its way upstairs, letting me know Mama was fixing those blueberry pancakes we all loved.

Ray-Jay was now twelve years old; full of vim and

vigor. When he asked Mama and Daddy if he could take the paper route in our neighborhood, and they said yes, he was like a different person, especially on Saturday. He had asked Daddy to drive him to pick up his paper bundle early so we could all have breakfast together.

After eating and cleaning the kitchen, Daddy left to attend a meeting at church. Ray-Jay, to everyone's surprise, asked Mama, "Can we hear some more about Uncle Tripe's adventures. Carl said his Uncle Joe was cousin to a famous cowboy who wrestled bulls at the rodeo."

"Why Ray-Jay, I'm happy you want to hear more about your Uncle Tripe, but his story is different from cowboys wrestling bulls. Your uncle was brave in other ways, when it came to his family, especially Grandma Sally and Papa Smith."

"Oh, yes," said Ray-Jay, "I like hearing about them. Are they in the story?"

"Yes," said Mama, leading the way into the family room and heading for her comfortable leather chair. Ray-Jay, Rickey and I got out our old beanbags and made ourselves comfortable. She began:

"It was one of the times when we were visiting Mama and Papa that I overheard a conversation between Tripe and Papa.

"I don't have a good feeling about all those big trucks showing up on Mr. Procter's land," Tripe said. "Before long, they'll be asking us to sell them some of our property."

Tripe had finished Morehouse College and worked for Atlanta Life Insurance Company as an accountant. He met Nellie there, and they were married a few years later. Nellie was a nurse who was pretty and very smart. They lived in Atlanta with your cousins, Jonathan and Thomas, until Tripe went missing.

Curious, I opened the screen door and walked out.

"Did I hear Mr. Procter's name?" I asked, easing myself into a nearby chair. "Is it okay if I listen in?"

Tripe looked at me and laughed. "Well, I don't know, Fannie. Promise you'll just listen and not get preachy on us?"

Papa didn't say anything, just grunted and took out his pipe, filled it with tobacco, lit it, and settled back in the old worn-out rocker we'd given him for his birthday many years ago.

"Mr. Procter owns a lot of land around here", Tripe said.

"Yep," Papa said, taking a long puff on his pipe.

"I remember watching men and women, boys and girls grow bent from back-breaking years of sharecropping. Working from sun up to sun down, and still not earning enough money to make ends meet at the end of harvest time. A new balance sheet at Procter's Market always showing a larger increase in their debt. It made him a very rich and powerful man," Tripe said, with a bit of anger in his voice.

"Yep," Papa said, taking his time sucking in, then blowing out billowy smoke from his pipe.

"The conditions most of them worked under were

down right criminal," Tripe said. "Mr. Procter was quick-tempered and rough with just about everybody." Pausing, he said slowly, "Everybody except you, Papa. Why didn't we sharecrop for Mr. Procter?"

Papa stopped puffing on his pipe, eased it from his mouth, and placed it on the little table beside him. "Now don't you go and get all fired up 'cause of something maybe you heard when you were a young'un," Papa said. Staring at Tripe with a steady gaze he said, in a soft voice, "Folks whispered that I was in his bloodline, going back to slavery time. Anyways, before Paw-Paw and Granny Vee. jumped the broom, old Mr. Procter up and gave him 24 acres of land. Some of the other nearby white farmers didn't like it, but nobody crossed Mr. Procter." Chuckling, he said, "Rumor was that he was a moody, conflicted man who worked his sharecroppers very hard and smiled kindly on those who worked their fingers to the bone."

A few months after that conversation, Tripe called to tell me what happened when he was there to check on Papa and Mama, as he did at least once a week. He said the three of them were sitting on the porch enjoying the evening breeze, after one of Mama's soul-satisfying dinners. Papa and Tripe content, communicating, as they often did, without words. Mama's body swayed in rhythm with the squeaking porch swing Papa had hung years before. Suddenly, their peace and quiet was interrupted by the screeching tires of a big, black truck that stopped in front of the house.

"Howdy, ya'll," said one of the three white men

getting out of the truck. Puffing on a cigar, he walked toward the porch, while the other two moved slowly around the yard, as if they owned it. Papa stirred to get up. Tripe said to him quietly, "Stay put."

With a worried look on his face, Papa whispered back, "Watch your tongue, Tripe. I see trouble ahead." Mama left to go inside.

Tripe stood up and walked to the edge of the porch.

"What can I do for you?" he asked, with a fake smile.

"Not what you can do for me, but what I can for you," he said, with a trace of irritation on his face—no doubt because Papa did not stand in his presence. "I hear this is Smith property, and I'm supposing that's your Pappy sitting down."

The fake smile gone, Tripe said, "You're right. This is the Smith family's property, and this is my father, John Smith".

The man looked at Tripe and then at Papa. "I'm looking to buy land," he said smiling. "And you, John, could be a rich man, if you're willing to let go of the land that runs past the pond until you reach the old mill."

Tripe said flat out, "This land will never be for sale".

The man with the cigar looked at Tripe a long time before saying, "Never say never." Then he turned, beckoned to the two men, and they left.

A few weeks later, one of Mr. Procter's sons up and sold land adjacent to our land, and before long, shotgun houses started popping up. Tripe told me when he heard about it, he put up a fence, blocking the view of the houses underway, and consequently the view of the *pond. The next year, Tripe went on a business trip to California and disappeared—just dropped out of sight."*

With that, Mama ended our history lesson, leaving open a floodgate of questions that dogged me for years.

Milestones Upon Milestones!

It was 1955. I hurried upstairs to get the beautiful bracelet Elsie had given me as a graduation gift. I was giddy with excitement and happy as a lark that Elsie and her little family were home for my graduation from high school. Yes! I was an aunt, thanks to Elsie and Victor. Little Victor was just six months old and Elsie beamed each time pictures were taken of them. She had found her dream while still employed with Miss Jackson. Daddy and Mama had always encouraged Elsie in her interest to be a teacher when she grew up. They finally accepted her decision to attend a small college in Columbus where she received an associate degree in retail management. After she graduated, Miss Jackson hired her to manager her store until she sold it. The realtor who sold the property turned out to be a Victor Livingston. In sharing the details with me, Elsie said Miss Jackson approached her about a customer who was coming in to exchange a gift he had purchased for his mother, and wanted her to help him in his search for the perfect gift. The long and short of it, both of them later agreed, was there were two perfects gifts exchanged that day.

Time was running out on me to decide which college I felt would best suit me, and after pouring over the brochures of those recommended by family and friends, Spellman College in Atlanta, Georgia was my choice.

The day I was packing to leave for college, Mama came into my room. She walked around touching pictures, picking up and putting down favorite things I had to leave behind. I said nothing, allowing her to feel whatever she needed for the moment. She sat on the edge of my bed. With a smile, I thought about how, when I was a kid growing up, there was no sitting on a made-up bed. Fondly, I watched her spread her hand over the covers.

"The nest will be almost empty when you leave for college, Kandi," she said, looking at me steadily. "There is a teeny part of me that would like to keep the nest full, but I can't and wouldn't; otherwise, how would either of you ever know how far you could spread your wings, as you prepare for travel on your own in your generation. That being the case, your Daddy and I are preparing for it." I went to her and we hugged each other for comfort.

My freshman year was not easy because I missed my family so much, especially Mama and Daddy, and adjusting to college was hectic in that I had to make, at times, decisions on the spot. It took a while, but I finally made up my mind to major in English and minor in Library Science.

Mama kept me up on news of the family. Rickey

had been drafted into the Army, and while he was excited about it, the rest of the family was not.

Ray-Jay was growing up like a weed. He turned out to be a good student and down to earth in his thinking—most times. Mama said he liked junior high school, and that math and biology were his favorite courses. Though he'd had a few unpleasant incidents with some of his schoolmates, she said he hadn't gotten into any kind of serious trouble. Primarily, she said, were those times when he tried to mediate angry situations between his friends or face-off with playground bullies taking advantage of kids afraid of them.

Near the end my sophomore year, I was hurrying to the library, when I stumbled and dropped my books; They went flying out of my reach. After picking up the last one, there in front of me was our newspaper carrier holding a pad.

"Here you go, Kandi," he said. At first, I was really embarrassed, but his deep voice put me at ease when he asked, "Are you hurt?"

"N-No," I said, angry with myself for stuttering. "I guess my pad flew out when I fell." I regained my composure, thanked him and rushed away with a quick good-bye. Once inside the building, I looked back and he was gone.

The next time I saw him was in the cafeteria at school. As an elective that semester, I had chosen an elocution class and was sitting alone reading over a paper I had to present in class.

When he came through the door, I believe we saw each other at the same time. He waved and came over to ask if he could join me, once he got his lunch. I said he could, but afterwards, I was so nervous, I wished I hadn't. Didn't he see I was sitting alone studying and maybe didn't want anyone to bother me, or I had finished my lunch and was about to leave? Tennyson, where are you? I said to myself. Before I could be rescued, he, not Tennyson, was at my table, and, as if reading my mind, said, "Are you sure it's okay for me to join you? It looks as though you are really into what you are studying."

Smiling, and moving my books and papers aside, I said, "Oh, no. Please have a seat. It's good to meet you again, after my little mishap on my way to the library. This gives me the opportunity to properly thank you for coming to my rescue. Amazed at the articulation that flowed from my mouth, I said, under my breath, as he settled in his seat, "Hmm, Mr. Tennyson, you can stay where you are, I don't believe I need you today!"

As we conversed, I learned that he was still at the seminary school in Atlanta, working on a Master of Divinity Degree. He said he often ate lunch at our cafeteria because the food was better and that the extra walk gave him a chance to clear his mind before his next class.

"What class is that?" I asked.

"Dr. Oullette's Elocution class," he answered.

I almost stammered, but, remembering Mr. Tennyson, I paused briefly before saying, casually, "I'm taking a beginner's elocution class from Dr. Harvey Ouellette. Are we speaking of the same person?"

"Why, yes," he said. "Dr. Ouellette teaches an advanced class at the seminary Tuesday afternoons."

"My class meets Tuesday and Thursday mornings," I said, irritated that I couldn't remember his first name.

"What a coincidence," he said smiling. "Maybe we can have lunch from time to time and compare notes." Holding up a thick notebook, he said, "This keeps me busy way into the night. I might need a little refresher from you," he said laughing.

There before me, in large letters, was his full name on the notebook. "Oh, I don't know about that, Sidney." We looked at each other and started laughing. Busted! I said to myself.

All too soon, it was time for both of us to get to our classes. I was pleasantly surprised when he came around to pull out my chair for me. With my things gathered securely in my arms, I said good-bye. He answered, "Until the next time, which I hope will be soon."

By the end of the semester, we had become friends—sharing and gathering information about our classes, ourselves and whatever topics of interest we wandered into, always knowing that our friendship was blossoming into something more.

We exchanged addresses, phone numbers and schedules—all leading to our first date. It was to a movie on campus, which we walked to. After the movie, we walked back to the dorm holding hands, laughing and giggling about insignificant things, until he suddenly stopped, and led me to a campus bench, where we sat down. Looking intently at me, he said, "I would like to speak to your father the next time I'm home for a visit."

Curious and somewhat surprised, I asked, "What for?"

"You mean you don't have any idea?"

I shook my head no and began thinking that maybe I didn't want to know.

"To ask permission to court you," he said.

Dating would be new territory for me. Not that I hadn't thought about it. Wasn't it every girl's dream to be swept off her feet by the love of her life? That's what I got from the books and magazines Elsie left laying around during our growing up days, but I never obsessed over it.

Hinged and Unhinged

It was the beginning of 1959, the year I graduated from college. On the horizon was the making of events that would be game changers in our country for a long time: The Vietnam War, though it was not called that at first, and the protest movement that was riveted with the electrified murmurings of young Black students at predominately Black colleges and universities. They knew that real, positive change and survival were the triggers in our salvation as a people and as a country. We were the next generation; our sense of self-worth, and self-preservation, were continually rocked and knocked about by daily headlines revealing the extent certain elements would go to keep their false sense of supremacy over people who didn't look like them—Negros, in particular.

The hateful, brutal murder of 14-year-old Emmett Till, in 1955, by a group of white male individuals in Mississippi; the sneakiness of those in southern towns who spilled hatred with their gasoline cans burning down black churches late at night; the cowardice in bombing the church in Birmingham, Alabama that killed two little girls attending Sunday school. These and other heinous acts of terror, revealed people who were devoid of one single strip of humanness. The results: the sit-ins, the marches, and the spread of other forms of protest within the Black community who spoke clearly with one voice, "Enough is enough!"

A few months before graduating from college, I took the Civil Service Exam and, to my surprise, was offered a job at the D.C. Public Library in Washington, D.C. as a library assistant. Daddy and Mama were unhappy with my decision to accept it, as I had been offered a scholarship to Atlanta University, but my heart was set on taking a break from school. The University gave me a one-year grace period to take advantage of the offer.

Sidney had received his Master of Divinity Degree and was offered a job as pastor of a small church just outside of Atlanta. He decided to take it and wanted to know my thoughts. I shared my situation with him and we agreed that we would give ourselves two years in the workforce before taking the next step in our relationship.

I had mixed emotions about moving to D.C. but the urge to forge ahead was greater than my doubts. After a few months, I grew to like my job among the books. Besides that, being independent felt great. Sidney and I talked at least twice a week. Though we missed each other terribly, we kept our resolve and stuck to our plan.

One morning, while waiting at the bus stop, I noticed someone who looked familiar. She came up to me, peered into my eyes and said, "You look like someone I knew from my childhood. What's your name?"

I was so taken aback by her manner, I couldn't believe I stammered slightly.

With a mischievous gleam in her eyes, she shot back, "Cat got your tongue, or don't you remember your name?"

"Jessie Mae? Oh, my God! It's you!"

We were so excited and so busy becoming reacquainted, we almost missed the bus. It was not crowded, so we were able to sit together.

Jessie Mae asked, "How long have you been in Washington?

"This is my second month. Jessie Mae," I said, "I thought I would never see you again after you left to go back to Alabama. Where do you live?"

"Right now, I live and work in a private home as a nurse and companion for Sarah and Lawrence Mackie. Both are lawyers by profession. Sarah befriended me when she was traveling in Alabama looking for someone to take over the primary care of her husband who was in a very bad accident. They needed live-in help for an indeterminate length of time. I had completed therapy and needed something different to refocus my life after Louise's death.

I said, "I'm so sorry, Jessie Mae. What happened to her?"

"I'm not sure you want to know, Kandi. It's a horrible story. For the longest of time, I couldn't talk about it without losing it, and was in therapy for over two years before I could function." Looking out the window, she said, "I get off at the next stop. Let's have lunch one Saturday and we can catch up. Saturday is my day off, unless there is a problem and I can't get away."

"Come to my place," I said quickly. "I'll fix lunch. Bring a dessert, if you like. I live in northeast D.C. in a cute little efficiency apartment just right for me." We exchanged addresses and phone numbers, just as the bus was slowing down at her stop.

Although surprised and happy to see my friend, Jessie Mae, her appearance spoke sadly to whatever the impact was of losing her sister. My heart was heavy with concern for her well-being.

When I didn't hear from her in several days, I called to say hello and find out whether or not she could make lunch the coming Saturday. She said she would let me know.

It turned out to be a month before Jessie Mae and I could get together for lunch. She shared that her employers were scared they were going to lose her, since she had met an old friend. She asked if I could stop by to meet them the following day after work. I did. Later, she told me I had passed the litmus test.

Our Saturday lunch finally rolled around. After eating and cleaning the kitchen, we headed for the davenport to relax and do some catching up. It was easy at first, sharing past snapshots of ourselves, not as easy now that we are different people, in different places, with different situations that brought us together in a chance meeting at the bus stop, after so many years.

"Louise didn't deserve what happened to her," Jessie Mae said softly, struggling for control. I allowed her time to recover.

"Jessie Mae," I said, "if it's too hard to talk about Louise, you don't have to."

"No," she said. "Just bear with me. Everybody knew that old Lucifer Silver, one of the two taxi drivers in town, was the last person to see her alive. Most of the whites believed his side of the story that she wanted to be dropped off to meet someone before going to the restaurant. Most of the people in the Negro community who knew Louise were wary of that explanation. Why Grandma let her go to the restaurant that time of night alone, I'll never know. She cried buckets of tears every day, asking herself that same question, until she died, a month after Louise was found. My mother blamed herself for not bringing Louise to Ohio with us. My on-again-off-again dad even got into the act, wanting to take me from Mama for what he called her bad judgment."

"What broke the case," I asked hesitantly.

"A headband and a sandal," she said, a wry expression on her face. Louise was smart in figuring out things and especially people. What must have gone through her mind when she realized what that evil, old dried-up poor excuse for a human being was going to do to her. Apparently, she fought to the bitter end to save herself, but was no match for his evil intent.

When he finished his low-down, dirty deed, he bashed her head in with a big rock, leaving it next to her body in that old make-shift cave—the scene of his monstrous crime."

I had so many questions going through my mind, but I felt she needed to get through the telling without interruptions.

She continued...

Days and weeks searching for Louise were to no avail. Lucifer, thinking he had escaped punishment, became careless while working in his backyard. A week-long spell of very hot weather caused him to shed the long-sleeved shirt he had worn to cover the many scratches and teeth marks on his chest and arms, unaware of the eyes of his neighbor's handyman. It was a Sunday morning, another hot, steaming day, when a Mexican farmer's tethered calf slipped his rope and wandered away. In search of it, he smelled an awful odor, not too far from where his animal had strayed. Following the odor into the partially covered cave, he found Louise's badly decomposed body. The news spread like wildfire, eventually bringing an unsettling closure between the Negro and white communities. Some of the whites believed Lucifer's story, that his cat caused the scratches and bites.

A tip to the police about Lucifer's scratches resulted in a search of his taxi. Pushed out of sight, under the back seat, was Louise's favorite headband stuffed in the sandal she had left behind. Did he go to jail for his deed? Of course not! He eventually lost his taxi business because few whites and no blacks at all used his taxi.

Sighing, and shaking her head, Jessie Mae said sadly, "I guess there will always be whites who can't accept the fact that the intentional loss of life of a black person at the hands of a white person deserves equal punishment as prescribed by law.

After she finished, we sat still, our silent tears evidence of the anguish we shared. She came over to where I was sitting, reached for my hands and held them tightly. She thanked me for listening and, in a quiet voice, said, "It's time for me to go. I'll be in touch with you, Kandi. I promise I will. My present job has helped me financially and spiritually, as I've worked through some very tough times."

There was a trace of the young Jessie Mae who made me laugh, when she chuckled and said, "I bet you didn't know that I can, at times, fly about on my wings."

That night, I called Sidney and shared the pleasure Jessie Mae and I had filling in the gaps of our lives, since parting so many years ago. I didn't mention Louise. Another day, another time, I said to myself.

Moments of Bliss and Sadness

A year passed since my brief reunion with Jessie Mae. We kept in touch from time to time, but our busy lives went in different directions. The winter months found her in Florida or California, where Sarah and Lawrence Mackie had summer homes, and I was in constant contact with my family. In a few years, Ray-Jay would be leaving the nest for college.

I loved my job at the library. It wasn't long before I received a promotion that placed me in charge of the Youth Division. Though it was challenging working with different age levels, I enjoyed going to work each day, especially on those days when the elementary children and I had special projects. My mom had wanted Elsie to teach school, but she got married instead. Maybe teaching was intended for me, I thought to myself.

When I talked to Sidney about it, he said, "You'd better start thinking fast...one year down and one more to go for us." We both laughed, looking forward to the next step we'd agreed to take in our relationship. I called Mama and Daddy that night to check on them, as I did once a week. When I brought up the teacher idea, they both were happy. But it didn't work out that way, not by a long shot.

It was the first day of fall and I'd had a good day at work. The phone rang just as I was coming in. When I answered, it was Sidney.

"I heard from Uncle Sam today," he said in a strained voice.

"Oh, no!" I said, knowing it meant he was being drafted into the army.

Sensing my dismay, he said in a calming voice, "Don't fret. We'll be happy for the extra time in the long run."

"You're right," I said, trying to match his cheerfulness.

Several weeks later, I flew to Atlanta and had the heartbreaking experience of watching him and other young men board the train for bootcamp, leaving family, friends, and sweethearts behind, knowing they would be in training to defend our country, and putting their lives in jeopardy, in case of war.

My job at the library kept me so busy, I found myself substituting a quick prayer for Sidney and Rickey, instead of worrying about the dangers they faced. It was always a joy to hear from Sidney, many times through his mom and dad, who were favorable to our budding relationship. After Sidney's eight weeks of training, I knew he could be sent anywhere in the world, especially with all the war murmurings that existed between our country and Vietnam. I was hoping it would be someplace in the States—not some faraway country.

Two weeks before Christmas, I went home to Texas to visit my family. Daddy and Mama were excited that all of us would be there for the holidays, even Elsie, Victor and baby Victor. Rickey, on a five-day leave from the Army, arrived Christmas Eve, and Ray-Jay, our little brother, now a high school senior, blessed us with his daily antics that kept us laughing. He told us, at our first breakfast together, that he had joined the anti-nickname club and now wanted to be called by his birthname, Raymond Jackson. When we all asked in unison why, he answered, "Because that's my name!" Thinking he was joking, we all laughed, including him, but I wondered if he was really trying to tell us something.

Unsettling News

Still wearing my warm and fuzzy feelings after being home with my family for the holidays, I was driving to work a few days later, thankful that I had passed my driving test and was finally able to own my first car. Humming a tune, I turned on the car radio. Not really listening, I continued humming until the words *escalation* and *war* caught my attention. Turning up the volume I heard the announcer say, "The United States is at war with Vietnam!"

The next few days gave everyone at work the jitters, even though some of the older employees said the *conflict* had been around since 1959. However, the news was encouraging, stating it would be a short engagement and over soon because of our might and power. History later proved that to be wrong.

On my way to work another morning, the news gave casualty numbers of our troops. I was saddened, thinking about Sidney and Rickey. That evening, I called Mama to see if she had heard anything. She said Rickey had checked in to let them know he was fine.

A few nights later, I answered the phone and it was Sidney. I was so happy and so thankful. "I thought I would call so that lovely mind of yours don't slip off the track worrying," he said, chuckling. "And," he continued, "there will be times, when in the field, I won't be able to call or contact anyone back home."

I was relieved to hear from him and to know that he was okay. I shared with him that the mood in the country was one of optimism by some and gloom by others. I quickly moved from that conversation to tell him about my new car, and that I was thinking about taking a few courses in law. Pausing after each word, he asked, "You want to become a lawyer?"

"I'm not sure," I said rather meekly, sensing he didn't have a favorable opinion about it.

He hesitated, and said, "Kandi, if you want to become a lawyer, go for it. You second guess yourself too often in matters that are important to you. We can't always be certain that decisions we make in our lives will turn out in our favor or not, but if we don't give it a run, we never will accomplish anything. Some of us are destined to have a long life, some not, but we can't stop living because of that possibility—can we?"

"Wow! I thought you would not be in favor of my going in that direction—maybe because you didn't see it fitting into your future plans," I said, pleasingly surprised by his answer.

"Let's just wait and see what the future really holds for us," he said.

"I'm looking forward to finding out," I said.

Those words would come back to haunt me. Two weeks to the day of our conversation, Sidney's convoy was ambushed. No one survived.

The Numbness of Life

Mama tiptoed into my room to leave water and a small snack on the nightstand. It had been a month since the tragedy of losing Sidney and all the other brave young men whose lives had been cut short by a war no one really understood, especially us common folks.

"Mama," I said, "please stay."

She returned to my bedside, gathering me in her arms, as though I was that little girl of long ago who sought her out to ease whatever pain I might have had.

Softly she said, "You need to eat, Kandi. The body needs nourishment to survive, even though you may feel numbed and detached from it. It also knows your pain, because the mind has alerted all systems that something is wrong, but it is the heart that carries the loss most, for it has been broken by the tragic loss of a loved one."

Though tears filled my eyes, I felt stronger than I had since Sidney's funeral. I remembered vaguely seeing Mama and Daddy pack clothes in a suitcase, our getting on a plane and arriving in Texas. After that, a numbness set in that I didn't know how to handle. I found out later that Sidney's parents had gone into seclusion after his death. I wanted so much to go to them and help comfort them, but couldn't. My supervisor gave me some time off, but I was unable to function, so Mama and Daddy came and took me home.

Three weeks later, I was back in my apartment, feeling stronger after a call from Sidney's parents. They shared with me bits and pieces of their son's life as he grew up. They're trying to comfort me, I said to myself. I should be comforting them. In the end, we found comfort in each other. I knew why Sidney was such an humble, kind, and loving human being—it came through his parents.

It took me another several months to feel alive and normal again. I was back at work, and were it not for my contact with the children, my recovery would have taken a lot longer.

During the summer, I enrolled in one of the local colleges to take two law courses, and was pleasantly surprised how changing my focus made a difference in my outlook on life.

Mama called one evening to tell me Daddy had had a mild stroke. I could tell she was worried, even though she said he was getting better. I was on a plane the next day to check out things for myself.

Before I was to leave for home, Mama told me she had heard from Uncle Tripe's wife, Nellie, and there was news about him.

"Oh, my gosh," I said. "Is he alive?"

"That was my first question," Mama said. "When she didn't answer right away, I figured he had died, and she was struggling with it, so I told her she could share details with me later. When I asked if she was alright, she said, "I have to go now, Fannie. I'll call you back later."

"This sounds as mysterious as Uncle Tripe going missing all these years. What about Johnathan and Thomas? They should be grown up now," I said.

"Well, it's hard to know how they have fared. When Tripe went missing, Nellie and the boys stayed in Atlanta, waiting to see whether or not Tripe would one day come home. We all tried to help her as much as possible. Then, she decided to move back to Chicago, to be close to her family. We were sorry to see them go, but supported her in the move. When she called the other day, she said she was going to California to visit Johnathan and his family."

"What about Thomas?" I asked. "Is he also in California?"

In a tired, weepy voice she said, "He's in prison in Alabama."

"My goodness, Nellie, what happened?"

"Let's go back in time and move forward to now," she said. That's when she told me how things went down with my brother.

"Tripe was down checking on your Mom and Dad when those guys in the pickup truck drove up looking to buy some of Daddy Smith's property. Actually, they were there to check out the lay of the land to report to someone else the chances of them buying the land or

getting the land some other way. Tripe being in the picture was a problem, especially since he said the land would never be sold.

When he returned home, he started receiving threatening mail, and phone calls. Also, people began watching his house. Knowing Tripe, he went to the authorities and reported what was happening. Since they gave only lip service to the situation, Tripe decided to do his own investigation. He was smart about it. Being in the insurance business, he had contacts from several sources that could help him. When he was advised by one source that he had become a target, Tripe went underground, so to speak. Traveling a lot on his job helped. While in California on business with the company, he went missing.

I nearly went crazy with worry and fear for the kids, after the first year and no word from Tripe. I went to the authorities and they said they had people looking into it. When I was asked by one of the investigators if maybe Tripe had taken off with another woman, I was done. That's when I moved back home to Chicago with the boys.

Growing up without a father was hard on them. Thomas, so much like his father, got into little scrapes now and then, but nothing serious. The day he called to tell me he had been picked up as a suspect in a serious crime, I was devastated. He said he had been set up and didn't know why because he was nowhere near where the crime took place. With little money for a good lawyer and his past scrapes with the law, he didn't have a chance.

I held on — living by a thread, until the day I got that letter in the mail. The handwriting was like that of Tripe's. My hands shaking, I ripped it open, nearly passing out when I read it. Tripe was alive!

It was the old, blind black man who begged for money near the cigar store who told Rev. Garrison, your parents' minister, that a lynching was going to take place to get rid of a high-minded, you-know-what from Atlanta who forgot his place in the presence of white people. One of the men in the group said it might not be a good idea, considering it was one of John Smith's grandsons; however he was shouted down and warned to keep his mouth shut.

That night, several black men called Tripe and told him of the situation. They hatched the plan that Tripe would go missing, and that everyone in his family had to believe he was probably dead. They arranged for him to go from California to, of all places, a small town in Maine. If you're wondering how they did it, they had help.

After a few years, when things died down, Tripe wanted to return home to us, but when Thomas went to prison, he changed his mind because he felt it was retaliation by the person or persons who had something to do with wanting his father's land and wanting him lynched.

When I was informed of all of this, I was told that Tripe was in a nursing home, dying of cancer. Only you and the boys know this story. Johnathan and I went to visit him. After hearing this story, Johnathan insisted that his Dad come to California and live with him.

After Mama's shocker of a story about Uncle Tripe, I experienced another shift from within. On my flight home, I felt the comfort of the clear, blue sky above, without a cloud, but knew, once I landed, there was a road before me, though cluttered with obstacles, I had to take—and I did!

Getting into law school was my first big hurdle. I was actually discouraged by some universities I wanted to attend. I was told it would be too much of a challenge financially...and other considerations. With the money I was making and saving, and help from financial aid, I felt I could squeak through if I took on a part-time job.

I was home for about two weeks. The phone rang. It was Jessie Mae. She wanted know if I was free to have lunch with her. Excited to hear from my old friend again, I said, "Just tell me when and where and I'll be there!" I could hardly believe my eyes when I saw her. The weight of the sorrow and pain surrounding the tragedy of losing Louise seemed lifted, and before me was a beautiful, intelligent, articulate, and mature young woman, who was my friend.

"Now what's your name again," she asked with that knowing smile, as we sat down for lunch at the upscale restaurant she chose.

I answered, just as articulate, "Kandi Kane, Esq., one day," I added. "At your service, Madame!"

"I know," she said. "I've been tracking you."

"What do you mean, tracking me?"

"Well, let's settle down and order our drinks. Oh, by the way, do you partake of strong drinks?" she asked.

"Only wine, and that's for special occasions", I said.

"Well, this is one of those occasions. First, let's look at the menu to see if you would like an appetizer, then we'll go from there," she said.

"Since I've never eaten in a restaurant so fancy, with fancy prices to go with it, I'm going to let you lead me through the drinks and meals," I said laughing, but meaning every word.

She was great at doing just that, and the food was delicious. Following the meal, she shared the direction her life took after losing her sister.

"Completing high school, I worked my way through college, earning a BS in nursing from Tuskegee Institute. I went through some bad times, and after all those years since Louise's death, my life was still in a turmoil—an emotional roller coaster. I decided it was time to get some professional help.

"After considerable therapy, I went to work for the Mackies. I didn't really like them at first because of the great divide between us, and because the evil person responsible for Louise's death was white. I took the job primarily because I didn't want to live on the streets. I was polite but remained distant from them. My salary was the deciding factor in my decision to stay put, at least for several months.

"Thinking back on my feelings for them, I was

surprised they didn't give me the boot after two weeks. They didn't, and today, because of them, I'm very wealthy. Something happened along the way. Because of the way they treated me, I found myself changing. When my mother died after Louise's death, I felt lost and bewildered.

"It was during my third year that I began to feel a closeness to them, almost like they were family. They had no children, not even a niece or nephew. They were Europeans, whose parents had come to America looking for a better life.

"One day, we had a disagreement over a minor issue, and I let my nose get out of joint, figuratively speaking. I was packing my clothes to leave, when Ms. Sarah came into the room. She said to me, 'We're going to miss you Jessie Mae, and we're sorry about the crack in our relationship, because of a difference of opinion. You have been like a daughter to us, but if you need to leave, that's your decision. I'll call you a taxi to take you wherever you plan to go.'

"I have no place to go, I thought to myself. Our house was sold after my mother died. I was living with an aunt and uncle who did the best they could to help me, but were poor. Aunt Lilly said one day, 'I'm sorry, Jessie Mae, we don't have the money to send you to college. I know my sister wanted that for you.'

"As I turned and looked at Ms. Sarah, all the feelings I had hidden from them and myself gushed out in a rush of tears. She came to me and said softly, 'Jessie Mae, let's get your things back in those drawers.'

After that, my life changed. I knew I could love people again, even though our faces and features were different. This is the lesson I got from that experience, Kandi. Being good or bad is not assigned by color. Black people can be good or evil, as well as whites or any other people, whatever hue. We all have the propensity to love or hate, based on whatever we allow to grow inside of us.

"When Mr. Lawrence passed away, I stayed on with Ms. Sarah. One day she called me into her office, handed me a large official envelope and told me to open it in my room. I sat on the bed and opened it. This has to be a joke, I thought. Hearing a sound at my door, I looked up; she was standing there smiling, and as if reading my mind, said, 'It's for real, Jessie.' It was her will, leaving me everything; her entire estate. Kandi, what you see is a changed person who was bountifully blessed by acts of kindness and love that crossed cultural barriers and color lines. That was astonishing to me coming from the segregated south.

"Ms. Sarah also felt there was something special about you when you came to the house to meet them. Soon afterwards, she said, 'Your friend, Kandi…there's something of essence trapped inside her, waiting to be released. It might be good for you to shadow her.' I've kept up with you ever since. Now… let's see. How long will it take you to finish law school so you can handle my business and personal affairs?"

We laughed as she gathered her things to leave.

Five years have passed since that conversation. It

was my last day at the library and the day my life took an unexpected turn. As I was walking down the steps, I encountered a tall, rather handsome black man coming in the opposite direction. He smiled and said, "Miss Kane, I believe?"

"Yes," I replied.

"Very pleased to meet you. I'm Keaton Everton, the new Librarian. I hear that you are one of our best employees, and that today is your last day. I never like to lose good people. Is there any way I can change your mind, or is leaving a done deal?"

I was somewhat startled by his comments, but there was something rather engaging about him. After Sidney's death, I thought I wouldn't find another romantic interest for quite some time.

Surprising myself, I said, "Maybe; I'll be back tomorrow for the remainder of my belongings. Perhaps we can have coffee in the cafeteria. They have the best."

"It's a date. How about noon?"

"Noon is fine, but let's not consider it a date."

"If you say so," he said, laughing.

The next day, when I got to the cafeteria, I didn't see him. I saw Susan Wilson, a co-worker who was also the office match-maker. Her sights had been on me since Sidney died. She came over and sat down. "Girl, you're leaving this place at the wrong time."

"Why is that, Susan?"

"Our new boss. He's single, cute and also very nice. Oh, look. He's coming this way."

"Hi Susan," he said. "I see you and Ms. Kane are having lunch. May I join you? I've been trying to match names and faces, and being the new kid on the block, I'm finding lunch time is the ideal time."

"I'm sorry, Mr. Everton," Susan said, "my lunch break is about over." She winked at me and practically skipped away from the table. That was the beginning of our courtship, even though not a date.

Jessie Mae thought Keaton was the right choice for me. Over a period of time, she had more surprises for me. One day, she said she had to go to court to settle a problem she was having with a client, but that we could have lunch afterwards.

I thought it strange that she wanted me to accompany her to the judge's chambers, but I did. When the judge reeled around in her chair, the first thing that caught my attention was her fiery red hair. We looked at each other. Her smile was familiar. Her nameplate read, Penelope Anderson-Jones. Observing the question on my face, she said, "I never told you Penny was my nickname." Coming from behind her desk, we met and hugged and hugged. Hugs, tears, laughter, and love were the court order of the day!

Having both Penny and Jessie Mae back in my life was truly a gift from heaven. We met as often as possible, but trying to catch up and make up the years in between proved to be a bit daunting. Penny and I, in the middle of our careers, working around aging parents, and children. Penny, a single parent with a teenage son, Philip. Keaton and I with son Travis, age

12, and daughter, Anna Bell, age 10. While Jessie Mae didn't have any children, she was involved in community pursuits that helped those most in need.

Being a philanthropist, she sat on several boards, and was often asked to speak at functions for different causes. It was always good to see her when she needed advice on legal matters.

Into the Home Stretch

I was quite excited the day I received a letter from Elroy Brown, my old essay partner, now the mayor of Hillsborough. He was inviting me to be the keynote speaker at the town's annual *History in the Making* celebration. He stated that each year the celebration recognized a former graduate of the Hillsborough School system who had made a worthy contribution to society.

Sitting with my family, in an auditorium filled with a multiplicity of ethnicities, waiting to hear me speak, was surreal. Walking to the podium, I thought of Tennyson and smiled. I would conclude my speech by reading my recently published poem, *Monumental Sin*.

Monumental Sin

When did it all begin, this monumental sin,
This monumental sin against mankind?
When placing the culture of a people
Atop slavery's cruel steeple,
Amid puritanical songs
Serving only to uncover wrongs
Of the insanity of man's inhumanity to man.

Royaline B. Edwards

When did it all begin, this monumental sin,
This monumental sin against mankind?
When the color of one's skin,
Used by self-proclaimed men
To equate exterior with superior,
Oblivious of the interior
That reveals a soul that knows this sin
Can originate from deep within.

When did it all begin, this monumental sin,
This monument sin against mankind?
When the quest for money and power,
Bowed to those in their ivory tower,
Enhanced by greed and ill-gotten gain
Blinding eyes to others' poverty and pain.
Excuses aplenty down through the years
Dashing hopes amid unfettered tears.

Chains may clink, chains may link,
Chains may be broken,
If the right words are spoken,
But to chain the human spirit against
    its will to be free
Is tyranny at work for *all* the world to see.
When did it all begin, this monumental sin,
This monumental sin against mankind?

Acknowledgements

To my husband, Kelvin, for his never-ending love, patience, and encouragement in helping me see Kandi to the end; to individual family members and friends who always inquired about the status of Kandi; to Jan Fields, a mentor, who saw many drafts of Kandi; and to my friends in the Wayfarers writing group whose encouragement and constructive critiques kept me focused!

Royaline B. Edwards